EiGHT O'CLOCK CLASSES

EiGHT o'CLocK CLASSES

AND OTHER LiFE-THREATENING SiTUATioNS

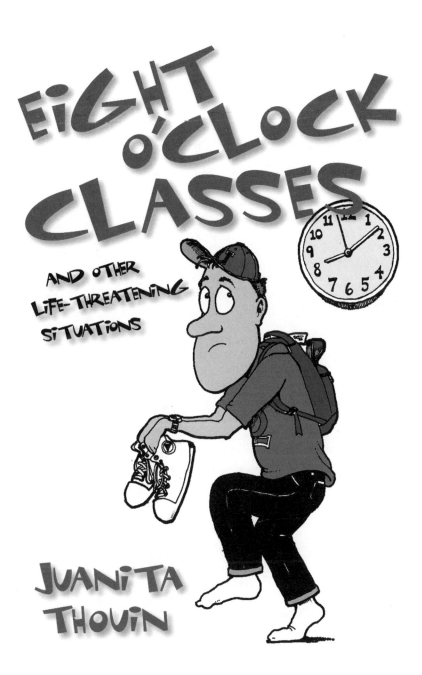

JUANiTA THoUiN

WINEPRESS WP PUBLISHING

Printed in the United States of America

Illustrations and cover drawing by Bryce Morgan
Editing by Steven R. Laube

ISBN 1-57921-104-6
Library of Congress Catalog Card Number: 98-60232

Acknowledgments

This book is dedicated to:

Mrs. Evelyn Kessner who spoon
fed me while I was a babe in Christ.
and to
Mrs. Aldeen Wenger, her faithful staff,
and the Bible Study Fellowship program
who taught me how to feed myself.

Special thanks to my husband Mark for always
supporting and encouraging my writing efforts.

Thanks also to noted author, John McCaleb, for his witty
sense of humor and wise counsel; to my son, Jesse, for allowing me to expose a good bit of his personal life to you, the
reader; to my cousin, Wes, for editorial assistance; and to my
daughter Elizabeth, son Jamie, and friend Chanda, for their vital
input. To Mrs. Kaye Norris who edited my first efforts and
refused monetary compensation, thanks hardly seems adequate.

CONTENTS

Contents

Contents

Foreword

Our middle child's decision to complete his high school education a year early resulted in the simultaneous graduation of our two oldest children. The following fall, Jamie, our oldest son, went into the United States Navy and Jesse, having just turned seventeen, went off to college. With their departure, our house grew quiet and I grew restless. Shortly thereafter, it was decided that our youngest child, Elizabeth, and I would commute to school together—she to Eastern Mennonite High School and I to James Madison University. Thus I began an adventurous return (after a twenty year pit stop) to the world of academia.

Walking the Christian walk in my nice cozy world of church, family, and Christian friends, presented little challenge to my faith. I soon found, however, that the real test of my identity was to come on the campus and in the classrooms of that university. Before long, I stopped hounding my college son regarding things about which I previously had no clue. It's true, that old Indian saying, "Don't judge a man until you've walked a mile in his moccasins."

Well, after three years, I've gained a great deal of respect for you young people who daily confront the stresses of discovering your identity and the real meaning of self-discipline. In addition to these "growing pains", you are saddled with mountains of studying, research, writing, and other academic baggage required to obtain the prize for which all college students press forward—a degree. Not surprisingly, you rise to the challenge with the vigor of youth . . . and shed your innocence in the process.

For the Christian student this metamorphosis includes breaking away from your parents' faith and embracing your own; internal and external assaults upon your beliefs make the passage all the more harrowing. Having witnessed this struggle first hand, *Eight O'Clock Classes* is my attempt to unmask some of these assaults and to share wisdom gained through ten years of intensive Bible training. Within these pages may you find joy, instruction, and encouragement!

For *His* glory!

—*mm*—

LIVING IN THE DANGER ZONE

Man does not live on bread alone, but on every word that comes from the mouth of God (Matthew 4:4).

Seek *first* the kingdom of God and His righteousness and all these things will be added to you as well (Matthew 6:33, paraphrased, italics added).

For out of the overflow of the heart the mouth speaks (Matthew 12:34).

When another student grabbed the parking space I was after, a four letter word flew out of my mouth. Of course, he couldn't hear me but I was appalled at who I'd become. Keeping up with the mountains of assigned reading and research papers left little time for anything else, including devotional time with God. And . . . it showed.

The body must be replenished with food and water and the spirit replenished with the Word of God. When we allow our defenses to weaken then Satan can easily gain a foothold. Just as we must expend the time and energy to fix ourselves something to eat and then eat it, so must we make a conscious effort to spend time with God; *nothing* is more important than our relationship with Him.

Occasionally, deadlines *still* kept me from spending time with our Lord. But after two or three more incidents like the one above, I was *very* careful to never let more than a day go by without seeking Him first.

How many days has it been since you last read the Scriptures or spent time in meaningful prayer?

For further reflection:
How can we know if we're being adequately fed? Read Galations 5:16-23.

—— 2 ——

⁓⁓⁓

FRESH STARTS

He has granted us new life to rebuild the house of our God and repair its ruins (Ezra 9:9).

Forget the former things; do not dwell on the past. See, I am doing a new thing! (Isaiah 43:18-19).

If anyone is in Christ, he is a new creation; the old has gone, the new has come! (2 Corinthians 5:17).

Before returning to college, I was basically a stay-at-home mom. (I did some substitute-teaching in my spare time.) That made me fair game for every volunteer organization that asked for help. Before long I assumed leadership roles in so many enterprises I've lost count, and became the initiator, chief cook, and bottle washer of a 4-H club, middle school career program, and county wide Youth for Christ organization (God gave me a 50/50 partner on this one.) I feel privileged that the Lord found me worthy of such contributions to Himself and community, but when an acquaintance phoned and asked me to start a private school, I was dumbstruck. How did I get such an overrated reputation?!

No matter who we are — child, teen, or adult — we acquire reputations (deserved or not) from those who know us or know about us. For some, our reputations are halos above the head; others live with balls and chains wrapped around the feet.

Going away to college presents the perfect opportunity to shake unwanted "notoriety". It's like starting all over again. This past year I met a brilliant, very likable student who shared, during a group study session, that he'd hung with the wrong crowd during high school, had committed a crime, and served time in detention. His confession totally blew us away! This guy was the epitome of a fresh start. Despite this confession, our perception of him did not change. We continued to regard him as a studious, brilliant, regular kind of guy because that's what we saw every day.

Simply changing the scenery does not change a reputation; actions must be altered as well. That doesn't mean becoming a fake by putting on a mask. Instead, with God's help, we can draw upon those natural qualities which have heretofore remained aloof or buried and/or lay unwanted baggage aside.

How about you? Would you like to change your image and become a new person? Now's your chance!

For further reflection:

The Israelites, known as slaves in Egypt, later gained reputations as mighty conquerors. How were they able to do this? Read Exodus 17:8-15 and Joshua 8:1-7.

THE FRESHMAN BLUES

The Lord had said to Abram, "Leave your country, your people and your father's household and go to the land I will show you" (Genesis 12:1).

Praise to the Lord who has not left you without a kinsman-redeemer . . . He will renew your life and sustain you (Ruth 4:14–15).

See I am sending an angel ahead of you to guard you along the way and to bring you to the place I have prepared (Exodus 23:20).

I will never forget my son, Jesse's, first day of college. The dorm was abuzz with students, parents, and siblings hauling clothes, stereos, computers, snack food, mementos, and an array of other necessary items into lifeless cubicles that were, right before our very eyes, being transformed into homes away from home. The air crackled with excitement but apprehension hung just around the corner.

Finally the moment we'd been anticipating arrived. Of course there was a barrage of last minute parental advice . . . then silence. Then, as we stood on the sidewalk in front of Miller Hall, my seventeen year old son hugged me tight and with a slight catch in his throat said, "I love you Mom. Thanks for everything." In the next instant he exclaimed, "Gotta go!" With a heavy heart I watched him turn and walk quickly away.

Two days later when I returned to Messiah College with the clothes we'd left hanging in the hall closet, Jesse confided in me that at the first night's dorm meeting a lot of guys had cried and several were really suffering from homesickness.

Going away to college serves as one way of cutting the apron strings. And anytime a severing of this sort occurs, there is bound to be heartache—for everyone. The ordained order of God is that we must eventually leave the shelter of the nest. He has prepared an exciting future for each of us and promises that when the leave-taking arrives, we do not go alone; He's always there.

We ran up outrageous phone bills and added many miles to our car that first year. However, as time passed the separations became easier and easier. Now, when Jesse returns home for holidays and summer break, only a few days elapse before the freedom of being "on his own" sings its siren song.

If you are experiencing homesickness, hang in there. God *is* with you and *will* sustain you!

For further reflection:
For comfort in this time of longing read Psalms 61 & 86.

SUDDENLY — FREEDOM

You, my brothers, were called to be free. But do not use your freedom to indulge the sinful nature (Galatians 5:13).

But solid food is for the mature, who by constant use have trained themselves to distinguish good from evil (Hebrews 5:14).

My son do not forget my teaching, but keep my commands in your heart, for they will prolong your life many years and bring you prosperity (Proverbs 3:1–2).

Acquaintances of ours, both committed Christians who raised their children under godly principles, were shocked one day when they opened a certified letter informing them of their car insurance's cancellation. The letter went on to explain that this family now posed too great a risk since their son, a college freshman, had had his license revoked for traveling at an excessively high rate of speed—a fact he "failed to mention".

Jesse, my son, decided to cut class for two days to indulge in an impromptu excursion to Mardi Gras. As it turned out, he was unexpectedly delayed by an ice storm and forced to miss three days of class instead of the intended two. To make matters worse, he missed an evening of work as well. Being so far behind in his studies and knowing that he let his boss down resulted in more than one headache in the days to follow.

Going away to college is a little like being a bird let out of a cage. Suddenly, the boundaries seemingly disappear and you are free to fly anywhere you want. But hidden dangers and tempting snares abound. Failure to heed the teachings handed down by loving parents and an omniscient God will likely result in pain (or worse) for yourself and those you love.

With freedom comes responsibility, and responsibility comes with maturity. Are you handling your newfound freedom in a mature manner?

For further reflection:
How can you be truly free? Read Psalms 119:44-48.

$\longrightarrow$

DON'T PRESS THAT BUTTON!

Make sure that nobody pays back wrong for wrong, but always try to be kind to each other and to everyone else (1 Thessalonians 5:15).

Bear with each other and forgive whatever grievances you may have against one another. Forgive as the Lord forgave you (Colossians 3:13).

Let us therefore make every effort to do what leads to peace and to mutual edification (Romans 14:19).

R oommate. Now there's a word capable of striking both excitement and apprehension into a prospective college student, and warmth or dread into any student who's already crossed that bridge. Without question, unless you commute to college from your parents' home, or live with the blessing of independent wealth, you *will* have to deal with the ups and downs of sharing a space that is *never* big enough, with someone raised differently than you.

Jesse lived on campus and in a dorm room for two years. He had several roommates, many of whom he now calls lifelong friends. However, for him, being a roommate entailed surviving: being kept awake *all night* by guitar playing; finding his snack drawer raided;

living with the humiliation of wrecking his roommate's truck and dropping another's portable CD player; clutter (he's fairly neat); constant television droning (he watches very little TV); and other petty nuances. On the flip side, he enjoyed being able to borrow a calculator when his disappeared for the moment; having someone *willing* to loan him a truck; having someone who could artfully fence parents' questions as to his whereabouts; and someone with whom to share his most private thoughts or pressing concerns.

The following words of wisdom, paraphrased from God's big book of instruction, can go a long way in making your rooming experience a more pleasant one.

- Be kind. Do unto your roommate as you would have him/ her do unto you. (Matthew 22:39).
- Sit down with your roomy and find out what "presses his/ her button". Then do your best to avoid those aggravations. (Romans 14:19).
- If there's a conflict, talk it out. Do not let the sun go down on your anger. (Ephesians 4:26).
- Forgive over and over again. (Matthew 18:21-22).

The way of following Christ means entering a life of sacrifice— especially when it comes to relationships with other people. So, how sacrificial have you been lately?

For further reflection:
According to Jesus, what is the crowning sacrifice of friendship? Read John 15:13.

—*mm*—

FAILURE AHEAD

How can they know if they have not heard? (Romans 10:14 para-phrased).

Study to show thyself approved unto God (2 Timothy 2:15 KJV).

The Holy Spirit . . . will remind you of everything I have said to you (John 14:26).

I wanted to take a class entitled "Audio Devices for Musicians". However, two prerequisites were required. The department head agreed to waive the first prerequisite if I could obtain at least a C in the other—the "Physics of Musical Sound". Piece of cake—right? Wrong! Within one week I felt totally lost and scored a 48% on my first exam. Believe me; I was desperate.

In my cry to God, the above scriptures came to mind. Using them as a springboard, I developed the following plan:

- Arrange a weekly study session with other students who were just as desperate as I.
- Tape record every lecture and while listening to the tape, make liberal use of the rewind and playback buttons.

- Never miss class! Never miss class! Never miss class!
- Pray diligently and ask God to help me, during tests, to recall all that I had studied.

God's faithfulness proved true and when my final grade arrived at semester's end, I was ecstatic to learn I had received a B in this class.

For further reflection:
Does God really care about the little details of your and my life? Read Matthew 10:30-31.

———*mm*———

TO BUY OR NOT TO BUY

He said to them, "But now if you have a purse, take it, and also a bag; and if you don't have a sword, *sell your cloak and buy one*" (Luke 22:36 italics added).

Ten virgins went out to meet the bridegroom. (Who was on his way to take them to the wedding feast.) Five of them were foolish and five were wise. The foolish ones took their lamps but did not take any oil with them. The wise, however, took oil in jars along with their lamps (Matthew 25:1-4 paraphrased).

Then all the virgins . . . trimmed their lamps. The foolish ones said to the wise, "Give us some of your oil; our lamps are going out." "No," they replied, "there may not be enough for both us and you. Instead, go to those who sell oil and buy some for yourselves." But while they were out buying the oil, the bridegroom arrived and the five who were prepared went with him (Matthew 25:6-10 paraphrased).

It was final exam week at James Madison University. While waiting for a friend outside of our campus center, I overheard the following conversation:

"Hey Jim! How's it going?"
"Not too bad."

"How'd you do on the psych exam?"

"Uh. Well. Brian and I were sharing a book for the semester and you know how that goes."

Though Jim and my son, Jesse, attend different colleges, they once shared a common bond. In an effort to have him understand the tremendous cost of an education, we required Jesse to purchase his own textbooks. At first, he saw no reason to part with hard earned money for something he could just borrow from the guy next door. For two years he failed to buy his own general education course books and for two years suffered through those classes like a bird trying to fly with clipped wings.

Certain tasks require certain tools and at times, it's foolish to assume that the job can be done with borrowed equipment. Adequate preparation for any assignment necessitates forethought and occasionally, a purchase made through sacrifice as well.

Having experienced, once too often, the pitfalls of attempting to share a textbook, Jesse, at last, decided to shell out the cash and buy his own books.

Whether you are a seasoned student or just getting started, the parable of the ten virgins contains a lesson for all: when exam time approaches, one book is not enough to go around.

For further reflection:
Is God capable of supplying exactly what you need even when there is no hope in sight? Read Exodus 16:11-18.

WHO AM I?

But each man has his own gift from God; one has this gift; another has that (1 Corinthians 7:7).

The Lord does not look at the things man looks at. Man looks at the outward appearance but the Lord looks at the heart (1 Samuel 16:7).

This is the confidence we have in approaching God: that if we ask anything according to His will, He hears us (1 John 5:14).

I thought I had it all together. Since I enjoyed writing and saw it as a personal strong point, I chose Journalism as a major. However as the college year progressed, questions arose: "Do I really qualify for this job? Who am I anyway, and is this what God wants me to do for the rest of my life?"

These natural questions come at various turning points in our lives. The transition from teenager to adult creates one of those points and the empty nest experience yields another; both are equally traumatic. Those of us who cling to God as our life support can survive this time with fewer bumps and bruises if we will remember to Whom our questions need be directed.

God created each of us with specialized, innate, abilities and gifts which correspond with His perfect will for our lives. Often times though, as in the case of David the shepherd boy (who eventually became king, see 1 Samuel 16:1-13), only God sees these attributes. So when we begin to struggle with our identity, we must *first* look to Him.

Pour out your confusions and ask the Father to give you a clear picture of His plan for your life. He *will* give you peace *and* direct your paths (see Proverbs 3:5-6).

For further reflection:
When did God formulate the plan for your life? Read Jeremiah 1:5.

—*um*—

WHO AM I? PART 2

To one He gave five talents of money, to another two talents and to another one talent, each according to his ability (Matthew 25:15).

For this reason I remind you to fan into flame the gift of God, which is in you through the laying on of my hands (2 Timothy 1:6).

The way of a fool seems right to him, but a wise man listens to advice (Proverbs 12:15).

Sometimes God speaks to us through human ambassadors: teachers, pastors, parents, experienced persons, friends, etc. When faced with difficult questions such as, "Who am I?" and "What am I supposed to do with my life?", it's often advisable to seek counsel from one or more of these individuals.

Listed below is some practical advice, garnered from several wise sources, which can help us through the identity crisis.

- Pray daily for guidance. Ask God to reveal any qualities which maybe visible only to Him.

- Make a list of specific abilities, gifts, and talents. Be honest and don't list any want-to-be's. (Unless, without question, directed by God to do so.)
- Visit the college career center. Inquire about an aptitude test.
- Select some careers which can best utilize newly discovered and previously known attributes. Then take survey classes for these, or do own investigating.
- Finally, if we are allowing God to direct our paths then we must follow our hearts—for therein lives our mighty counselor, the Holy Spirit.

For further reflection:
Does God orchestrate the events of our life in accordance with His will? Read Proverbs 16:9.

~mm~

MAJOR PARENT DILEMMA

But each man has his own gift from God; one has this gift, another has that (1 Corinthians 7:7).

Honor your father and your mother, so that you may live long in the land the Lord your God is giving you (Exodus 20:12).

The son will not share the guilt of the father, nor will the father share the guilt of the son . . . I will judge you, each one according to his ways (Ezekiel 18:20,30).

Julie, one of my college friends, accepted a volunteer leader position with a local Christian ministry for teens. She loved the work and turned out to be a dynamic leader. Therefore, she was quite despondent when her parents said, "no" to a major in Youth Ministry.

Jon*, my son Jesse's roommate, wanted a career in music. His parents wanted him to have a nice secure future and "strongly suggested" a major in Biology. Out of despair, he rarely attended classes and did not return for the second semester.

When you and your parents don't agree, choosing a major can be a real time of turmoil. On the one hand, you must honor your parents . . . on the other hand you are your own person, uniquely created by and responsible to God.

If you are facing a similar dilemma, I suggest the following:

- Pray that God will change your parents' hearts. Again I say, pray!
- Even Christian parents have a hard time discerning the fine line between giving guidance and direction and forcing what we think is best upon our children. Draw up a game plan stating exactly: what makes you suited to this particular career; why and how you feel called by God; what hope there is for financial independence(and if there isn't any, how you will supplement the income); and what it will take to achieve your goal. Then, sit down face to face and present this to your parents.
- If you are still at an impasse then perhaps some Biblical wisdom is in order. In 1 Samuel 17:15 we see that David, out of respect for his father, spent part of his time in the service of Saul and the other part taking care of his father's needs. In short, he compromised. Perhaps you can compromise by double majoring or minoring in the field of your choice.
- If there is still a conflict, counseling with your pastor may help.
- If no solution can be found then consider the possibility that you are trying to enact *your* will and not God's.

For further reflection:

Was Jesus ever in conflict with His parents and if so, how did He handle it? Read Luke 2:41-52 and John 2:3-10.

---

*Jon and his parents eventually came to a merging of the minds. After graduating from Full Sail Real World Education (school of recorded arts) with a degree in sound engineering, he headed to Nashville and has since worked for such notables as Code of Ethics, Audio Adrenaline, Newsboys, and DC Talk.

mm

PASS THE SALT PLEASE

So do not be ashamed to testify about our Lord (2 Timothy 1:8).

Be wise in the way you act towards outsiders; make the most of every opportunity. Let your conversation always be full of grace, seasoned with salt, so that you may know how to answer everyone (Colossians 4:5-6).

After they prayed . . . they were all filled with the Holy Spirit and spoke the word of God boldly . . . in Jerusalem, and in all Judea and Samaria, and to the ends of the earth (Acts 4:31 and 1:8).

Since I'm not the kind of person who can walk right up to strangers and share with them the four spiritual laws,* I wear T-shirts and sweatshirts which display various Christian messages. In doing so, others know, right up front, that I'm one of those "Jesus people". In this simple, quiet way I've not only shared some truths about the gospel but offered an open door for anyone who might have questions about spiritual matters—and many have taken the bait.

On the first morning of my return to the world of academia, much to my surprise and consternation, I hesitated when reaching for the T-shirt which read, "Jesus is the Way, the Truth, and the

Life." Fear and apprehension paralyzed me; there was just something very intimidating about baring my soul to a group of persons who I thought would snicker and sneer. For several seconds, as I stood in indecision, a battle raged within. In the end I resisted the devil, he fled, and I wore the shirt. But, in those few short moments I realized that my faith was about to be tested as never before.

All who have come to know Jesus as their personal Savior are expected to share the life changing message of the gospel with any who will listen. Mostly we do this by the example of how we live our lives. But, we also do it by openly testifying about the Good News. The boldness to speak forth this truth comes from the power of the Holy Spirit which Christ gave us. By choice we either allow that power to flow or we squelch it.

In the early weeks of that first semester I fought many similar battles but soon learned that I didn't need to be afraid. Though some (students and professors alike) stared holes through me, others found me a "safe" haven for conversations about their Christian upbringing and a few even asked questions about the Bible. Nearly all, though they may have disagreed with my beliefs, treated me with respect.

Are you too intimidated to share your faith? Call upon the power of the Holy Spirit, resist the devil, and boldly become Christ's ambassador to the ends of the earth!

For further reflection:
What kind of power do we have through the Holy Spirit? Read Ephesians 1:19-20.

---

* A very effective witnessing plan developed by the founder of Campus Crusade for Christ International. See *Witnessing Without Fear* by Bill Bright, Chapter 9

mm

RESPECT

Each of you should look not only to your own interests, but also to the interests of others (Philippians 2:4).

Honor your father and mother . . . that it may go well with you and that you may enjoy long life on earth (Ephesians 6:2-3).

Each of you must respect his mother and father (Leviticus 19:3).

My son, Jesse, a college sophomore in Pennsylvania at the time, decided to cut class for two days and head for the glitz and glitter of Mardi Gras. Of course, he knew better than to consult his parents first; a less than desirable GPA spelled certain disapproval of such a plan. What he didn't bargain for was our impromptu call to the dorm during his absence.

We left a message on his voice mail for him to call us back— protocol for a parent trying to reach a student. When he failed to respond we were a little miffed but still nonchalant. However, after 30 hours and several vain attempts to make contact, we were a *lot* more than miffed; we were sick with worry. His roommate finally returned our frantic messages and informed us that our son had gone to a "jazz festival" somewhere. (A clever way of beating around the bush.)

Of course, everything turned out all right. He's still alive and well but had to live without his car for the remainder of the semester. We acted amazingly cool about the situation, ourselves having made rash choices in pursuit of adventure. But I can tell you, being on the parent end was no fun at all; it was scary!

No man is an island. Nearly all of us have *someone* who concerns him/ herself with our well-being. We are obliged to consider their feelings. And, if that caring person(s) happens to be our parents then there are other considerations as well, such as obedience and respect.

Who's paying for your education? Is it respectful to squander this money through poor grades? Irregardless of financial concerns, when did you last thank your parents or say, "I love you"?

For further reflection:
As we grow older, what does God require of us in relation to our parents? Read 1 Timothy 5:4,8.

—*mm*—

OFF BALANCE

They sow the wind and reap the whirlwind (Hosea 8:7).

All a man's ways seem innocent to him, but motives are weighed by the Lord (Proverbs 16:2).

Folly delights a man who lacks judgment, but a man of understanding keeps a straight course (Proverbs 15:21).

Towards the end of his Mardi Gras escapade, Jesse, and his companions, Brad and Sam, were stunned by a phone call from us, Jesse's parents. Our firm "suggestion" that Jesse swing by the house before returning to campus heightened their foreboding. Since the trio was traveling in Jesse's car, Brad and Sam had no choice but to ride along.

Arriving at our home several hours before we returned from work and school, the adventurers had plenty of time to sit and stew over the coming storm. Anxious to get back to campus and out of harm's way, Brad and Sam began to search around for some mode—any mode—of transportation that would make the one-hundred and thirty mile trip back to Messiah College. After several phone calls, they discovered that they weren't old enough to rent a car but *were* old enough to rent a moving van.

At the local rental depot, Sam and Brad plunked down $230 (via credit card), climbed into a 20ft. truck, and waved good-bye to Jesse. A few weeks later they mailed us a copy of the bill, secretly hoping we would take pity on a couple of poor college boys; we didn't.

Jesse gracefully accepted the loss of his automobile privileges. Unfortunately, an ice storm, which arrived shortly after Sam and Brad's departure, prevented us from returning him to college until the following afternoon thereby creating additional "headaches".

Every decision we make carries consequences. Sometimes they're pleasant; sometimes they cause suffering. The key to maximizing the pleasant consequences and minimizing the suffering is to check our motives and use sound judgment based on godly principles—in all we do.

What have you been reaping lately?

For further reflection:
What must be done after acting in folly? Read Psalms 38:5,6,18,21.

—*mm*—

IS HE OR ISN'T SHE?

Whoever has my commands and obeys them, he is the one who loves me (John 14:21).

The man who says, "I know him," but does not do what he commands is a liar and the truth is not in him. But if anyone obeys his word, God's love is truly made complete in him. This is how we know we are in him: Whoever claims to live in him must walk as Jesus did (1 John 2:4-6).

But the fruit of the Spirit is love, joy, peace, patience, kindness, goodness, faithfulness, gentleness and self-control . . . those who belong to Christ Jesus have crucified the sinful nature with its passions and desires (Galatians 5:22-24).

Julie volunteered in a Christian organization along with a guy named Doug. They enjoyed a playful, platonic relationship and soon became best friends. Eventually, their feelings for each other deepened, causing Julie great turmoil; God warns against becoming unequally yoked and although Doug claimed to be a Christian, his actions were inconsistent with such a claim.

Christians are not sinless. Satan constantly crouches at the door, tempting our carnal nature; regrettably we sometimes fall prey to his schemes. However, our *lifestyles* do not reflect an *unbridled pattern* of sin. Instead, when transgression comes, we who truly love the Lord cry out to Him with sincere and repentant hearts. Then, through those refining experiences, we find ourselves, *in increasing measure*, molded into the likeness of our Savior.

In love, every Christian ought to test the spirits—for our own benefit and the benefit of the pre-Christians around us. However, only by steeping ourselves in scripture can we discern those who already enjoy a personal relationship with the Lord from those who need our prayers for salvation. (Apart from a deep abiding relationship with Christ Jesus, there is no salvation, see John 14:6).

What about your friends? Are they or aren't they . . .

For further reflection:
Hypocritical judging or discernment? Read Luke 6:37-45.

uun

THE DATING GAME

For this reason a man will leave his father and mother and be united to his wife and they will become one flesh (Genesis 2:24).

Do not be yoked together with unbelievers (2 Corinthians 6:14).

A woman is bound to her husband as long as he lives. But if her husband dies, she is free to marry anyone she wishes, but *he must belong to the Lord* (1 Corinthians 7:39 italics added).

One of my college friends was so excited. After bounding through the door and declaring "You won't believe what just happened!" she gushed over a promising encounter with a guy she had a crush on. Unintentionally, I popped her bubble by asking, "Is he a Christian?"

Jesse, my son, landed a date with a really "hot chick". Later he told me what a great time they'd had. In conversation, he casually mentioned her association with the wrong crowd. "But," he assured me "'deep down' she's a Christian."

Romantic love is as unpredictable as a summer storm and like lightning, cupid's bow often strikes when you least expect it. God admonishes Christians *not* to marry unbelievers and dating is frequently a prelude to marriage.

I am intimately acquainted with the hardship of being unequally yoked. For although I love my husband with whom I have been one flesh for twenty-five years, we don't see eye to eye on spiritual matters. The resulting difficulties often make my hair stand on end!

God does not give us commands to ruin all of our fun. Instead, He has provided a road map that, if followed, will guide us down life's highways and byways with the least amount of heartache.

Are you following God's road map in your dating practices?

For further reflection:
If you think you'll be able to bring your spouse to salvation after marriage, read 1 Corinthians 7:15-16.

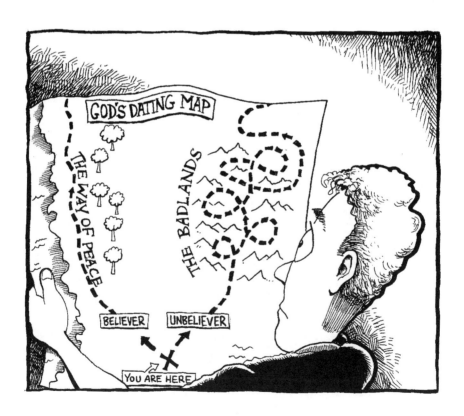

A FICKLE AFFAIR

As the Father has loved Me, so have I loved you. Now remain in my love (John 15:9).

Never will I leave you; never will I forsake you (Deuteronomy. 31:6).

For I am convinced that neither death nor life, neither angels nor demons, neither the present nor the future, nor any powers, neither height nor depth, nor anything else in all creation, will be able to separate us from the love of God that is in Christ Jesus our Lord (Romans 8:38).

Whenever I visit my college friends in their dorm rooms the conversation inevitably turns to the joys and woes of various relationships. Not only do we discuss who is dating whom but also how best friends have parted ways over some very painful misunderstanding.

Over the years I've shed my own fair share of tears due to the rejection of loved (or liked) ones. The truth is, friendship (more often than not) is a fickle affair. And as pat as it sounds, we can only count on one Person to be there for us—no matter what. His name is Jesus Christ, our forever friend.

Jesse writes music and has beautifully captured the pain and joy of this reality in a song entitled "Forever Love". The lyrics are as follows:

> I knew you were lonely. But you never told me
> Until today,
> When I saw you cryin'.
> You said, "would you hold me". And later you told me,
> You loved it so. When we held each other close.
>
> *chorus:*
> Will you love me tomorrow, I'll never know.
> But there's only One who will love me Forever.
> Forever Love.
>
> Three days later I couldn't wait to see your face again
> And share my feelings.
> But you weren't ready, to be going steady, with this lonely man.
> Now I've lost my only hope.
>
> Emptiness filled by God. Mercies from Heaven,
> We'll see from now on.
> A love that carries on Forever. Not like another love,
> Forever Love.
> (© 1993 Jesse Thouin)

For further reflection:
Read about the trouble King David had with his friends in Psalm 55:12-14 and how he responded in Psalms 63.

44

PITFALL

For the waywardness of the simple will kill them, and the complacency of fools will destroy them (Proverbs 1:32).

Remember this: Whoever sows sparingly will also reap sparingly, and whoever sows generously will also reap generously (2 Corinthians 9:6).

And whatever you do, whether in word or deed, do it all in the name of the Lord Jesus, giving thanks to God the Father through Him (Colossians 3:17).

When I was so miserably failing "The Physics of Musical Sound", I engaged another student in the class to tutor me. I chose an obviously bright young woman who had just changed her major from Physics to Music; it seemed a match made in heaven. Unfortunately, she lacked dedication and tried to rely on the book for knowledge rather than class attendance. When questioned about something specifically discussed during lecture she would often say, "Well, let me look that up and get back to you."

After about two weeks our tutoring sessions just sort of dissolved and I found other ways of acquiring help. Her sporadic attendance continued and it wasn't long before she didn't attend at all; I assume she dropped the class. (I have never met a student who could routinely cut class and still make the grade—let alone learn something.)

College represents an investment; *someone* is spending big bucks for your education. A single class cost me hundreds of dollars. I knew that if I put forth less than my best effort, I'd be squandering that much of God's money.

As Christians, *everything* we do serves as a witness for Jesus Christ—even how we approach our studies. Of course, we are human and there will be days when we find ourselves pressed for time or just completely exhausted. God understands that. But, constant misuse of His resources (time, money, brain) is indeed the mark of a fool.

For further reflection:
What happens to those identified as fools? Read Romans 1:21-32.

———*mm*—

Under the Covers

You must observe my Sabbaths. This will be a sign between me and you for generations to come, so you may know that I am the Lord, who makes you holy (Exodus 31:13).

There are six days when you may work, but the seventh day is a Sabbath of rest, a *day of sacred assembly*. You are not to do any work; *wherever you live*, it is a Sabbath to the Lord (Leviticus 23:3 italics included).

Let us not give up meeting together . . . but let us encourage one another—and all the more as you see the Day approaching (Hebrews 10:25).

It's been a tough week at school. You took two killer tests and completed a five page comparison and contrast assignment. On Saturday night you hang out with your friends until the wee hours of the morning and with only a slight twinge of guilt, pass by the alarm as you fall into bed. After all, Mom won't be there to raise her eyebrow when you crawl out from under the covers at 1:00PM. And, it won't hurt to miss church just one time.

The question is, how many "one times" have there been and when you do wake up how will you spend the rest of the day?

I can't tell you how many times I, myself, have been tempted in a similar scenario. Fortunately though, age and experience play in my favor; I'm a little more resistant to this particular temptation than I used to be.

Jesus said the Sabbath was made for man, not man for the Sabbath and I can attest to the validity of this statement. When we begin forsaking the assembling of ourselves together the following occurs:

- We feel like we're running around spiritually undressed for the rest of the week.
- After awhile, we become disconnected from the body of Christ.
- We become short-tempered.
- Eventually, even our devotions and prayer time slack off.
- We loose sight of who we are in Christ.
- Soon we become arrogant and self-centered.

Satan, a crafty fellow, claps his hands in glee every time we fail to honor the Sabbath and keep it holy because *he* knows that soon we'll loose sight of Who it is we serve *and* the righteousness that comes only from Him.

God did not give us commandments to put a damper on our lifestyle—but for our own good. Are you in the habit of staying in bed and turning down something good?

For further reflection:
What does it mean to keep the Sabbath Holy? Read Deuteronomy 5:12-15, Nehemiah 13:15-22, Matthew 12:9-12, and Colossians 3:15-17.

mm

EMPTY POCKETS

Set your mind on things above, not on earthly things (Colossians 3:2).

Keep your lives free from the love of money and be content with what you have (Hebrews 13:5).

Gold there is, and rubies in abundance, but lips that speak knowledge are a rare jewel (Proverbs 20:15).

It is no sin to be poor. I find this welcome knowledge because putting two through college and another through private high school certainly stretched our family budget.

During my first semester's return to life as a student, I tried to maintain a part-time job. But as the studies mounted, time became more valuable than money and soon that extra income went by the wayside. Now I eat packed lunches while sitting in my car, seldom buy CD's, scan the thrift shops for brand name clothing, and virtually have no social life.

For many traditional college students, foregoing a part-time job is not an option. Still, the pitiful amount earned from work study or part-time employment barely provides enough to keep up with the laundry, buy a few snacks, and join friends for a pizza blitz.

Continuing one's education in pursuit of a degree requires sacrifices of various kinds. For most, that repertoire definitely includes money. However, we must remember that God has a plan for our lives and empty pockets are simply a by-product of this temporal training ground. When we grumble and complain about our current circumstances we actually murmur against God and call into question His perfect will.

Do you complain about empty pockets or are you content with what the Father has given you?

For further reflection:
What happened to the Israelites when they grumbled against God? Read Numbers 11:18-20,31-34.

~~~

SLAVERY

Like a city whose walls are broken down is a man who lacks self-control (Proverbs 25:28).

Do not be a man who strikes hands in pledge or puts up security for debts; if you lack the means to pay, your very bed will be snatched from under you (Proverbs 22:26-27).

Make it your ambition to lead a quiet life, to mind your own business and to work with your hands . . . so that your daily life may win the respect of outsiders and *so that you will not be dependent on anybody* (1 Thessalonians 4:11-12 italics added).

Receiving mail is still an exciting part of the day. I suppose I should thank all of the credit card companies for filling my mailbox with letters offering "pre-approved" credit cards; at least I almost never walk away from the post office empty handed. But . . . don't these guys ever give up?!

American citizens are inundated with easy credit. We purchase cars, clothes, vacations, music, gasoline, and even food without having to shell out a dime—until the bill arrives. *Then* the truth sinks in: credit isn't so easy after all.

Cheryl applied for and received her pre-approved credit card shortly before Christmas. By the second week of January she'd racked up a hefty $500 in charges. Since her work study income is for tuition, upon returning from Christmas break, she desperately searched for an off-campus job. No more free time and no more impromptu visits to friends at other colleges. Now she must slave away at some grease joint to pay for the "effortless credit" and its interest.

Nearly all of us have been duped by the "easy credit" scheme . . . myself included. Yet, credit is not evil for those disciplined in its use. Non-cash purchases of durable goods such as an education or an automobile should be entered into with a clear, thoughtful approach to cost and income. However, purchases of nonessentials such as the latest fashion trends, dinner at the new steakhouse in town, or a just released, gotta have, CD, are better made with credit *only* if the money to pay the bill *already* sits in the checking account.

What about you? Are you maintaining self-control over your credit spending or are you like a city with broken down walls?

For further reflection:
What's the secret of being content with what we have? Read Philippians 4:12-13.

—um—

THE AGE-OLD LIE

"You will not surely die," the serpent said to the woman. "For God knows that when you eat of it your eyes will be opened, and you will be like God, knowing good and evil" (Genesis 3:4-5).

Son of man, say to the ruler of Tyre, "This is what the Sovereign Lord says: In the pride of your heart you say, 'I am a god' . . . but you are a man and not a god" (Ezekiel 28:2).

When the crowd saw what Paul had done, they shouted in the Lycaonian language, "The gods have come down to us in human form!" . . . the crowd wanted to offer sacrifices to them. But when the apostles Barnabas and Paul heard of this, they tore their clothes and rushed out into the crowd, shouting: "Men, why are you doing this? We too are only men, human like you" (Acts 14:11-15).

Quiz time! What do spiritualism, inner-self teachings, tree hugging, cults, sorcery, horoscopes, psychic readings, evolution, guided imagery, the other seven, major, world religions, and a myriad of psychological/scientific philosophies not mentioned here have in common? I'll let you contemplate that question for just a moment.

Now that you no longer live under the safety of your parents' spiritual wing, Satan plans to work overtime in order to draw you away from the Truth. How many times have you been tempted to pay a visit to the local palm reader? How many of your courses include teachings which ignore God's control of the universe and focus on man's spiritual, intellectual, and physical ability to solve personal or sociological problems? (Such as self-meditation rather then prayer as a means to reduce stress.) Does your college newspaper include weekly or daily horoscopes and do you read them? How many of your friends find the work of Gandhi more fascinating than the work of Jesus Christ?

Each of the above scenarios find their roots in the common thread eluded to in the quiz question. That common thread is this: *Each, in some way, deny or pervert the deity of God, the Father, Son, and Holy Spirit and elevate man (or other created things) to "god" status.*

Some label this recent interest in the created rather than the creator as "New Age". However, such perversion isn't new at all. In Romans 1:25 Paul, in speaking about those who reject God, said, "They exchanged the truth of God for a lie, and worshipped and served created things rather than the Creator—who is forever praised. Amen." And God warned of such deception thousands of years ago when He gave Moses the first of ten commandments— "You shall have no other gods before* me."

Satan does no less to assault *your* faith than he did to Eve just shortly after creation. So whenever you come into contact with any philosophy, teaching, or religion which calls into question God's truths or His deity—stay alert—Satan lurks just around the corner!

For further reflection:
How can we know the difference between God's truths and Satan's lies? Read Psalm 119:9-16.

---

* NIV text note indicates that an alternate translation for this particular word is "besides".

mm

EVERY MAN FOR HIMSELF

For none of us lives to himself alone (Romans 14:7).

Each of you should look not only to your own interests, but also to the interests of others (Philippians 2:4).

And He died for all, that those who live should no longer live for themselves but for Him who died for them (2 Corinthians 5:15).

I was quite taken aback one day when I realized that my prayers of late were less and less for others and more and more for myself. Spending nearly every waking hour selecting and attending classes in preparation for a lifelong career caused me to focus an inordinate amount of time on the question, "Who am I, really?".

The college setting naturally lends itself to self-exploration. But allowing this necessary process of inner reflection to steal away my Christlike concern for others posed a serious threat to my spiritual health. God calls Christians to place the interests of others high on the priority list. To help maintain the balance between "me and thee", I found the following activities helpful:

- Each day, pray for one other person besides myself.
- Whether it be as simple as smiling at a stranger or as elaborate as taking a friend's work shift in the cafeteria so he can study for an exam, don't go to bed at night without having done at least one good deed for the day.
- Get involved a service organization either on or off campus.

For further reflection:
Who deserves praise for the good things you do? Read 2 Peter 3:14-15.

—*wm*—

VALUES CLARIFICATION?

Do not think that I have come to abolish the Law or the Prophets; I have not come to abolish them but to fulfill them (Matthew 5:17).

Do we then nullify the law by this faith? Not at all! Rather we uphold the law (Romans 3:31).

"Why do you ask me about what is good?" Jesus replied. "There is only One who is good. If you want to enter life, obey the commandments" (Matthew 19:17).

Ever since manmade governments began eliminating the Ten Commandments from the walls of schools, public buildings, and from textbooks, today's social gurus have had a field day with a philosophy they label "values clarification".

Christians need not and must not toy with the idea that individuals possess the right or responsibility to determine their own set of values. *Our* moral laws were defined, thousands of years ago, by the finger of God upon two clay tablets. They read as follows:

- I am the Lord your God . . . you shall have no other gods before me.

- You shall not make for yourself an idol in the form of anything in heaven above or on the earth beneath or in the waters below. You shall not bow down to them or worship them . . .
- You shall not misuse the name of the Lord your God, for the Lord your God will not hold anyone guiltless who misuses his name.
- Remember the Sabbath day by keeping it holy. Six days you shall labor but the seventh day is a Sabbath to the Lord your God.
- Honor your father and mother . . .
- You shall not murder.
- You shall not commit adultery.
- You shall not steal.
- You shall not give false testimony.
- You shall not covet . . . anything that belongs to your neighbor.

Are you clarifying your values through the Word of God?

For further reflection:
What was Jesus' response to the question, "Teacher, which is the greatest commandment in the Law?" Read Matthew 22:36-40.

———*mm*———

VITAMIN FORTIFIED

Don't you know that you yourselves are God's temple and that God's Spirit lives in you? (1 Corinthians 3:16).

If anyone destroys God's temple, God will destroy him; for God's temple is sacred, and you are that temple (1 Corinthians 3:17).

Do you not know that your body is a temple of the Holy Spirit? . . . You are not your own; you were bought with a price. Therefore honor God with your body (1 Corinthians 6:19-20).

I took an 8:00AM computer literacy course last semester. Fun! Apparently, one of the instructor's pet peeves was nutrition. More than once he asked for a show of hands from everyone who had eaten breakfast. Each time, out of thirty or so students, three lonely hands went up.

During our family's college shopping days, I found it amusing that at every school we visited, the tour director never failed to point out the numerous brands of cereal served at each and every meal. I've since learned that this vitamin fortified, 101 variety, quick to eat "breakfast" treat is the mainstay of every student's diet, including mine. When my husband leaves for out of town business, Elizabeth and I eat cereal for dinner.

College students are notorious for skipping meals, eating on the run, avoiding vegetables, and foregoing a balanced diet. Sometimes we do so because a scheduled class conflicts with mealtimes; sometimes laziness plays a role; sometimes we're broke and buy what we know is cheap and will fill us up. But the real, inexcusable, reason for our unhealthy eating patterns remains undisciplined care of God's spiritual temples.

Throughout history God has been very adamant about the structure, care, and use of His temple; as sacred ground it must be treated as such. In the book of Exodus, God explained in *great* detail how the Israelites should set up the tabernacle, how the furnishings would look, and who would manage the affairs of this great sanctuary. And, in the book of Matthew we see Jesus chasing the merchants and money changers out of the temple in Jerusalem because they were desecrating it.

God cares about His spiritual temples as well. Through Paul, He admonishes us to treat our bodies with the respect deserved as dwellings of the Holy Spirit; what we do or do not put into our bodies matters.

Sometimes we have no choice as to what we will eat; other times we do. When we do, we ought to bear in mind our accountability for those choices.

God won't come down and strike us with lightning if we eat a whole bag of licorice once in awhile or occasionally eat cereal for dinner. But when we constantly ignore our body's nutritional needs, He may chase out the desecration by landing us at the doctor's office or worse yet, in a hospital.

What has your diet consisted of lately?

For further reflection:
Our earthly bodies are temporal. What kind of a body will we have in eternity? Read 1 Corinthians 15:35-44,49 and Matthew 17:2.

25

GOING GREEK?

Do not be yoked together with unbelievers. For what do righteousness and wickedness have in common? Or what fellowship can light have with darkness? What harmony is there between Christ and Belial? What does a believer have in common with an unbeliever? (2 Corinthians 6:14-15).

For you spent enough time in the past doing what pagans choose to do—living in debauchery, lust, drunkenness, orgies, carousing and detestable idolatry. They think it strange that you do not plunge with them into the same flood of dissipation, and they heap abuse on you (1 Peter 4:3-4).

Do not love the world or anything in the world. If anyone loves the world, the love of the Father is not in him (1 John 2:15).

Upon graduation from high school, I attended Miami University (of Ohio). Shortly after classes began, I received several notices regarding rush periods for various sororities. I did visit one of these show and tell parties but ultimately decided the Greek-letter society just wasn't my style.

To most people, mentioning the words fraternity or sorority brings to mind images of free-flowing alcohol and immoral behavior. Sadly, this image may be more fact than fiction (depending on the mindset of your local chapter) for many Greek social organizations. And Christian students have no business yoking themselves with those who tolerate these kinds of activities. However, not all Greek-letter societies fall into the social category thereby prompting us to use caution in stereotyping all fraternities/sororities.

For those ignorant of the Greek society structure, there are four kinds of fraternities/sororities: social, professional, honor, and recognition. Professional fraternity membership is limited to persons majoring in or pursuing specific careers. e.g. education or law. Honor fraternities are for those with high GPAs. And recognition fraternity membership is limited to those with outstanding achievements in a specific arena, such as community service.

The easiest way to lead godly lives is to avoid entanglement with persons or things which tempt us to sin. God reiterates this truism over and over throughout scripture. When considering involvement in any organization, *Greek or non-Greek*, we who claim the name of Christ should carefully consider how such membership might influence our Christian walk. One way of doing so is by asking ourselves the following questions:

- Does this organization promote morals and values compatible with mine?
- Are the activities promoted by this organization in keeping with activities acceptable to God?
- Will membership in this organization yoke me closely together with other members and if so are they kind of people God wants me to keep company with?
- Will the time commitment required for involvement in this organization prevent me from cultivating my relationship with Jesus Christ?

An honor fraternity recently invited me to join their ranks. At some point I may contemplate their offer but right now I just don't have the time. Are you thinking of going Greek? Have you carefully considered how membership in the sorority/fraternity will affect your Christian walk?

For further reflection:
Why should we perfect holiness in our lives? Read 2 Corinthians 7:1.

—*mm*—

THE $64,000 QUESTION

Those who obey his commands live in him, and he in them. And this is how we know that he lives in us: We know it by the Spirit he gave us (1 John 3:24).

But the fruit of the Spirit is love, joy, peace, patience, kindness, goodness, faithfulness, gentleness and self-control (Galations 5:22-23).

For this very reason, make every effort to add to your faith goodness; and to goodness, knowledge; and to knowledge, self-control; and to self-control, perseverance; and to perseverance, godliness; and to godliness, brotherly kindness; and to brotherly kindness, love. For if you possess these qualities *in increasing measure*, they will keep you from being ineffective and unproductive in your knowledge of our Lord Jesus Christ (2 Peter 1:5-8).

We all struggle with questions pertaining to our identity: "Who am I?" "What do I want to do with the rest of my life?" "Who will I marry?" But the $64,000 question that nearly every Christian, at some point in time, seems to agonize over the most is: "Do I really belong to Jesus?"

Sin came into the world when Satan tempted Eve to doubt God's Word (see Genesis 3:1-7). Satan tried to turn Job away from God by tempting him to doubt God's goodness (see Job 1:6-11). Satan wants to make us ineffective spiritual losers by tempting us to doubt our salvation (see James 1:6).

In John 10:27-28 Jesus said, "My sheep listen to my voice; I know them and they follow me. I give them eternal life, and they shall never perish; *no one can snatch them out of my hand.*"

If you're asking the question, "Do I really belong to Jesus?" take note of the following: The fact that you are reading this devotional indicates that you want to follow Jesus. And if you have honestly confessed with your mouth and sincerely believe in your heart that Jesus is the Christ, then you *do* belong to Jesus (see Romans 10:9) and are sealed with the Holy Spirit (see Ephesians 1:13).

In case you can't get a grasp of anything so simple, read the scriptures at the top of this page and ask yourself, "Have I experienced spiritual growth? As time goes on, am I exhibiting more fruits of the spirit? Am I kinder than I used to be? Do I have more self-control? Do I understand more of the scriptures? Etc., etc." If your answer is yes, then tell Satan to take a hike. If your answer is, "no" or "I don't know", then pray right now. Ask Jesus to forgive your sins and come into your heart.

It's that simple . . . and that profound.

For further reflection:
Who called you into fellowship with the Savior and promises to keep you strong to the end? Read 1 Corinthians 1:8-9.

———

SLEEPING AROUND?

But among you there must not be even a hint of sexual immorality, or of any kind of impurity (Ephesians 5:3).

Marriage should be honored by all and the marriage bed be kept pure, for God will judge the adulterer *and all of the sexually immoral* (Hebrews 13:4 italics added).

It is God's will that you should be sanctified: that you should avoid sexual immorality; that each of you should *learn to control his own body* in a way that is holy and honorable, not in passionate lust like the heathen who do not know God; and that in this matter no one should wrong his brother or take advantage of him. The Lord will punish men for all such sins (1 Thessalonians 4:3-6 italics added).

When I graduated from high school and went off to college, the sexual revolution was in its infancy. Now, some twenty years later, it's in its prime. More than a few see chastity as some sort of plague and promiscuity as the social norm. Many educational institutions, always ready to embrace revolutionary ideas, now offer coed dorms with nearly unlimited visitation guidelines. If they do happen to post "no-visitation" hours, it's usually to ensure quality study time—not because administrators seek to discourage sexual encounters among unmarried students.

Undeniably, the human sex drive is a very powerful force. Also true: humans derive much pleasure from sexual intercourse. God ordained these truths in order that we might "be fruitful and multiply". However, sexual intercourse is also, undeniably, an intimate, bonding encounter wherein a man and woman become one flesh. Likewise, children (the fruit of this pleasurable experience) undeniably do better when raised within a two parent family unit. For these latter reasons, God commands that sexual activity occur *only* within the context of marriage.

God has not left those of us who claim the name as Christ as orphans. He fully understands the weakness of the flesh and mercifully empowers us with the Holy Spirit. By steering clear of compromising situations and calling upon that Holy Power we *can* and *must* maintain self-control over our driving sexual desires. To do otherwise finds us crossing the boundary into disobedience and sin.

Are you sleeping around with sexual immorality?

For further reflection:
Our Father is always willing to forgive those who offer true repentance for their sins. For confirmation regarding the compassion of God, read Luke 15:11-32.

—*mm*—

STICKS, STONES, & WORDS

He who covers over an offense promotes love, but whoever repeats the matter separates close friends (Proverbs 17:9).

A gossip betrays confidence; so avoid a man who talks too much (Proverbs 20:19).

They are full of envy, murder, strife, deceit and malice. They are *gossips*, slanderers, God-haters, insolent, arrogant and boastful . . . they are senseless, faithless, heartless, ruthless. Although they know *God's righteous decree that those who do such things deserve death*, they not only continue to do these very things but also approve of those who practice them (Romans 1:29-32 italics added).

L isa and I were casual acquaintances; she roomed with my friend Diana. One day I answered the phone to find a very distraught Lisa on the other end of the line. It seems she confided the possibility of an out-of-wedlock pregnancy to Diana and then later learned that Diana "confidentially" shared Lisa's predicament with at least five other people. Sensing I comprised one of the five, Lisa phoned to beg my silence.

Webster defines gossip as: a.) a person who habitually reveals personal or sensational facts b.) a rumor or report of an intimate or sensitive nature. Bear in mind, the definition indicates that *gossip can be the spreading of truth, as well as fiction.* Revealing a personal fact about someone constitutes gossip just as much as spreading a rumor.

Gossip not only separates close friends (which eventually happened to Lisa and Diana), it can absolutely destroy a person's reputation. As such, God deems gossip sin and likens this evil to murder.

Are you in the habit of destroying others with sticks, stones, or words?

For further reflection:
Is there ever a time when we should expose facts about someone else? Read Matthew 18:15-17, 1 Timothy 5:17-20 and Galations 6:1.

CHEERS!

Do not get drunk on wine which leads to debauchery. Instead, be filled with the Spirit (Ephesians 5:18).

Let us behave decently . . . not in orgies and *drunkenness*, not in sexual immorality and debauchery, not in dissension and jealousy. Rather clothe yourself with the Lord Jesus Christ, and do not think about how to gratify the desires of the sinful nature (Romans 13:13-14 italics added).

The end of all things is near. Therefore be clear minded and self-controlled so that you can pray (1 Peter 4:7).

I have only been "smashed" once in my life. It didn't happen intentionally and believe me, it never will again. I was young and really quite ignorant about the power of alcohol. My husband and I went to a dance with friends of ours, and they introduced me to strawberry daiquiris. Daiquiris don't taste like mixed drinks at all; they taste like fruit juice. Boy, I was sucking those icy delights down one right after the other! Suddenly, the liquor took effect and I found myself unable to talk. I tried to talk, and sounds that resembled words tumbled out, but it felt as though a great wad of cotton filled my mouth and I knew my garbled speech made no sense.

At this point in my life I was what I call a "seeker"—one who actively investigates and participates in Christianity but doesn't really know what it means to have a *relationship* with Jesus Christ. I certainly wasn't consciously aware of 1 Peter 4:7. But at that moment, when my mouth was "filled with cotton", a frightening thought entered my mind: "What if Jesus returns right now? I won't be able speak to Him and give an account of all I've done—good or bad."

Various denominations differ in their views on the acceptability of *moderate* amounts of alcoholic consumption. And some scriptures passages appear ambiguous on the subject. However, God clearly states that *drunkenness* is a trait of the wicked who will not inherit the kingdom of God (see 1 Corinthians 6:9-10).

College students, suddenly unleashed from childhood, often find themselves eager to engage in activities reserved for adults. Even students who have gone beyond the "seeker" stage and know Christ personally are tempted to experiment with alcoholic beverages. But to all I say, "Beware!" Christ may choose to return at any moment and it's impossible to be clear minded and intoxicated at the same time.

What kind of cheering will you be doing when Christ returns?

For further reflection:
For a dramatic rendering of Christ's return read 1 Thessalonians 4:16-5:8.

~mm~

SILVER AND GOLD

Wounds from a friend can be trusted . . . Do not forsake your friend or the friend of your father (Proverbs 27:6-10).

Then they kissed each other and wept together—but David wept the most. Jonathan said to David, "Go in peace, for we have sworn friendship with each other in the name of the Lord, saying, 'The Lord is witness between your descendants and my descendants forever.'" Then David left, and Jonathan went back to town (1 Samuel 20:41-42).

After this . . . Paul met a Jew named Aquila . . . and his wife Priscilla . . . and because he was a tentmaker as they were, he stayed and worked with them . . . for a year and a half (Acts 18:1-11).

For my daughter and I, traveling to our respective schools requires an eighty-four-mile daily commute. This, in addition to extracurricular activities, often keeps us out and about until late at night. Such an exhausting schedule has completely altered our social lives and sadly, left more than a few friendships hanging in the wind.

As we pass through the various stages of life, friendships bloom and fade. Leaving home to attend college certainly represents one of these stages. And, just as David and Jonathan felt the intense pain of parting, so might we in leaving behind our hometown confidants. However, also like David and Jonathan, we must recognize that, though they may change in nature, "sworn" friendships stand the test of time and separation.

I miss my trusted friends but find comfort in our occasional exchange of notes and phone calls. By the same token, embracing friendships on campus has afforded new opportunities for caring, sharing, and having fun.

What about your changing friendships? Are you embracing the new and trusting the wounds of the old?

For further reflection:
Should having only one or two close friends worry us? Read Proverbs 18:24.

FINDING FORGIVENESS

For what I want to do I do not do, but what I hate I do. I know that nothing good lives in...my sinful nature. For I have the desire to do what is good, but I cannot carry it out. For in my inner being I delight in God's law; but I see another law at work in the members of my body, waging war against the law of my mind and making me a prisoner of the law of sin . . . What a wretched man I am! Who will rescue me from this body of death? Thanks be to God—through Jesus Christ our Lord! (Romans 7:15,18,19, and 22-25).

On hearing this, Jesus said, "It is not the healthy who need a doctor, but the sick. But go and learn what this means: 'I desire mercy, not sacrifice,' For I have not come to call the righteous, but sinners" (Matthew 9:12-13).

If we confess our sins, he is faithful and just and will forgive us our sins and purify us from all unrighteousness (1 John 1:9).

Why can't I seem to get it right? Why do I find myself spreading gossip after vowing never to do so again? Why do I loose control when the fast food clerk messes up my order? Why do I allow time constraints to usurp opportunities to witness?

Why do I sling cutting remarks at my husband? Why don't I act like a Christian?!

The carnal nature belongs to Satan. The spiritual nature belongs to God. Therefore, while we go about our daily routines, a battle constantly wages between this evil and good (see Ephesians 6:10-18).

Satan employs an army of demons and owns an arsenal of weapons designed to prod us into disobedience against God. Sometimes our armor is firmly fitted and we deflect Satan's arrows with ease. Other times, our armor is askew and Satan gains the upper hand. When those later times occur, if we call out to Christ, He reaches down with a love we barely understand, forgives our sin, and puts us back into the battle. With each failed skirmish, we gain wisdom; the next time Satan attempts to employ that same tactic, we are more prepared. (Occasionally we *really* struggle with a particular sin.)

True perfection will only be realized when Christ returns to do final battle with Satan (see Philippians 3:12). Until then, the Holy Spirit helps us to fight the good fight of faith (see 1 Timothy 6:12) and Christ forgives us when we fail (see 1 John 2:1).

If you've blown it, do not despair. Christ's love is far reaching and His mercies everlasting. Come before your Savior, seek forgiveness, straighten your armor, and get back into the battle. Remember, "you are from God and have overcome Satan because the One who is in you is greater than the one who is in the world" (1 John 4:4).

For further reflection:
Is Christ's grace a license to keep on sinning? Read Romans 6:1-2, and 15-23.

———

HE'S TOUCHING ME!

I will not leave you as orphans; I will come to you (John 14:18).

Keep on loving each others as brothers (Hebrews 13:1).

You are to help your brothers . . . until they too have taken possession of the land that the Lord your God is giving them. After that you may go back and occupy your own land (Joshua 1:14).

It's been two years since our oldest son, Jamie, went into the U.S. Navy and middle child, Jesse, left home to attend college. For me, the initial shock of having our family miles apart has melted into a rather reluctant acceptance of the natural course of events. My husband, Mark, basks in the pleasantness of a tidier home, snacks that are still there when he wants them, and competing for computer use with only two people instead of four. However, Elizabeth, the lone remaining child at home, is *still* not a happy camper.

When her brothers come home on leave or for break, Elizabeth returns to her normal, exuberant, joy-filled self. When they depart, she mopes around the house like a sick puppy. When they phone, she lights up like a light bulb; after awhile, the light fizzles out. Though busy with friends, school, and playing basketball, the void created by Jamie and Jesse's absence remains constant.

Having a brother or sister leave home can be emotionally devastating for those siblings left behind. Not only has their homelife changed, often, their "best friend" has moved away. It's important that you recognize these transitional struggles and remain sensitive to your brother(s) or sister(s)' needs. To make the transition easier, I suggest the following:

- Pray for your sibling.
- Call or write to your sibling at least once a week.
- Show an interest in your sibling's life; remember birthdays, congratulate achievements, ask about friends.
- When you *are* home be certain to *make time* for your brothers and/or sisters.

A special bond will always exist between you and your siblings. And until the younger brothers and sisters reach maturity, for the older sibling there remains not only a bond but a certain measure of responsibility as well.

Have you recognized and accepted that responsibility?

For further reflection:
What is the true meaning of brotherly love? Read 1 John 3:16-17.

———*mm*—

THE HANDICAP CHALLENGE

Do not curse the deaf or put a stumbling block in front of the blind, but fear your God (Leviticus 19:14).

We who are strong ought to bear with the failings of the weak and not to please ourselves (Romans 15:1).

And we urge you brothers, warn those who are idle, encourage the timid, *help the weak*, be patient with everyone (1 Thessalonians 5:14 italics added).

Though not readily noticeable, I'm handicapped. Ten years ago the bus on which I traveled drove over a speed bump at the exact moment I was turned around talking to the person behind me. Voila! Whiplash. To this day, avoiding and/or managing the chronic pain requires constant vigilance. For this reason, carrying a school bag remains completely out of the question. I function as a commuter student by being the envied owner of a handicapped sticker which allows me to park nearby and carry only one book at a time to class.

Another commuter on campus drives a carload of students to school each morning and also owns an envied handicapped sticker. Only . . . he's not handicapped. I've never had the guts to ask him *how* he obtained that sticker but I did overhear him tell one of his passengers, "No, I don't feel guilty", when she sheepishly commented on their convenient parking spot.

God expects obedience from we, who claim the name of Christ, in life's simple encounters as well as the profound. Laughing at mentally challenged individuals, cursing a driver who's traveling too slow, or stealing a handicapped parking space may not seem like a big deal. But these actions are just as incompatible with the Christian walk as illicit sexual activity or shoplifting.

Pleasing self or bearing with the failings of the weak? Where do you stand?

For further reflection:
As the proponents of euthanasia advance their twisted, godless philosophies upon our society, how must Christians respond? Read Proverbs 31:8-9.

─⁓⁓─

HEY! ARE YOU LISTENING?

When you ask, you do not receive, because you ask with wrong motives, that you may spend what you get on your pleasures (James 4:3).

This is the confidence we have in approaching God: that if we ask anything *according to his will,* he hears us. And if we know that he hears us—whatever we ask—we know that we have what we asked of him (1 John 5:14 italics added).

Then Jesus told His disciples a parable to show them that they should always pray and not give up (Luke 18:1).

We serve an awesome creator—He numbered the very hairs of our head. We also serve a very loving Father—He picks us up when we fall. But most importantly: God always has our best interest at heart. For instance, you think that that gorgeous used car is just what you need to travel back and forth from home to school; He knows the owner lied about the mileage and that if you have a vehicle on campus your studies will suffer. I think that I really need another credit card because many places don't accept the one I currently possess; He knows that I'm not a disciplined credit card user and cash works just fine.

I often hear people whine and complain because they think God doesn't hear their prayers. Others label Him uncaring because prayers have gone unanswered. And a few actually reject Christianity altogether because they know so and so who prayed for such and such and didn't get it.

God is not a genie in a bottle. He is the Creator of the universe and the author of our soul. He is a God of order with a perfect plan for all creation—including your life and mine.

God *wants* to give you and I good things and in fact, blesses us abundantly; just having the financial resources to pursue a college education is a terrific blessing. Somehow though, when our idea of a good thing conflicts with God's idea of a good thing, we tend not to see the forest for the trees; we want what we want and grumble against Him for not giving it to us. We need to step back and remember: God sees the panoramic picture; we only see a snapshot.

If you have requests which go seemingly unheard:

- Check your motives.
- If they appear to be in accordance with scripture and what you believe His will to be . . .
- Be persistent and keep praying—my mother has a friend who prayed for her husband's salvation for forty years before he came to the Lord.

For further reflection:
There are unseen spiritual battles raging all around us and sometimes answers to our prayers are detained in the midst of these battles. Such was the case for Daniel as recorded in Daniel 10:12-14.

IT'S PARTY TIME!

Elisha went up to Bethel. As he was walking along the road, some youths came out of the town and jeered at him, "Go on up, you baldhead!" He turned around . . . and called down a curse on them in the name of the Lord. Then two bears came out of the woods and mauled forty-two of the youths (2 Kings 2:23-24).

For you have spent enough time in the past doing what pagans choose to do—living in debauchery, lust, drunkenness, orgies, carousing and detestable idolatry. They think it strange that you do not plunge with them into the same flood of dissipation, and they heap abuse on you. But they will have to give account to him who is ready to judge the living and the dead (1 Peter 4:3-4).

So whether you eat or drink or whatever you do, do it all for the glory of God (1 Corinthians 10:31).

Spring break! Hallelujah! Let's hit the road and not look back for seven wonderful, glorious days!

I never really understood the whole spring break thing until I started back to college. Now I know why Jesse wanted to cast his cares to the wind rather than come home and sit around the house. Yet, the psychology of this desire almost defies explanation; as I write I find it difficult to pen words which adequately describe the incredible feelings of restlessness and fatigue . . . the yearning for a grown-up recess. Even my three years as a department store clerk lend no insight; all those weeks and months at the same job never induced such emotion. When my shift terminated I went home and relaxed; the restlessness never had a chance to build. But as a student, the constant need to cram information into the memory bank never goes away; the pressure stays on my mind eighteen hours a day—as I drive, while I eat, in the grocery—always, the wheels are churning. Help! My brain needs a break!

Jesus understood the human need for times of respite. In Mark 6:31 He told His disciples, "Come with me by yourselves to a quiet place and get some rest."

According to Webster, the word rest can mean not only sleep or repose but renewed vigor and peace of mind or spirit. The original New Testament Greek word for "rest", *anapauo*, offers such meanings as refresh, wait, or take life easy. It sounds like spring break certainly fits God's blueprint for respite.

There's just one catch . . . while these activities synonymous with spring break *do* measure up to God's standards for righteous living, others such as drunkenness, carousing, vandalism, disrespect, and one night stands, do not.

Does this mean that we students who claim the name of Christ should sit home and twiddle our thumbs for seven days. Of course not! But it does behoove us to carefully consider where we will go to unwind, what activities we will engage in, and who our comrades will be.

So, what's up for your spring break? Will your party activities follow the way of pagans, or the way of God?

For further reflection:
When tempted, what should we do? Read James 4:7 and 1 Timothy 6:11.

~~~

EVERYONE'S DOING IT!

The world and its desires pass away but the man who does the will of God lives forever (1 John 2:17).

Do not conform any longer to the pattern of this world, but be transformed by the renewing of your mind (Romans 12:2).

Let no one deceive you with empty words, for because of such things God's wrath comes on those who are disobedient. Therefore do not be partners with them (Ephesians 5:6-7).

You've no doubt heard the old adage, "There's safety in numbers." For the most part that's true. Walking across campus late at night with a group of friends is certainly safer than crossing alone; standing in line to use the automatic teller machine makes one less of a target for thieves than having this "genie" all to oneself. But for we who claim the name of Christ, being counted among the majority is often a hindrance rather than a help.

Somehow, we've gotten the idea that if our peers are doing it, it must be okay—myself included. I've gossiped with friends, watched a movie that others warned was contrary to Christianity, disobeyed traffic laws, desecrated the Sabbath, etc., etc. all because . . . well . . . others were doing it.

The fact of the matter remains, God calls you and I to a higher standard and the world's ways are not usually our ways. Jesus said, "Wide is the gate . . . that leads to destruction and many enter through it. But . . . narrow is the road that leads to life, and only a few find it" (Matthew 7:13-14). He also taught that even though others lead me into sin, *I* am still accountable for that sin (see Genesis 3:17). And they are accountable for having led me astray (see Matthew 18:7).

Where have you found your safety lately? In obedience unto Christ or hangin' with the crowd?

For further reflection:
For a repertoire of behaviors which have no place in the life of a Christian, read Romans 1:28-32 and Galations 5:19-21.

mm

YES, YOU CAN!

I can do everything through Him who gives me strength (Philippians 4:13).

And we pray this in order that you may . . . be strengthened with all power according to his glorious might so that you may have great endurance (Colossians 1:10-11).

And God is able to make all grace abound to you, so that in all things at all times, having all that you need, you will abound in every good work (2 Corinthians 9:8).

It was spring semester. In addition to enrollment in the Bible Study Fellowship program, (the class and study time are equivalent to a three credit hour college course) I had registered for four courses at James Madison University, including a law class and a physics course. The academic load coupled with my daily ninety minute commute, and duties as mother and wife proved monstrous. Within two weeks I knew I was in over my head. But the deadline to drop without sacrificing any money had passed, so I decided to stick it out.

Dr. James Dobson once told a story about a family who captured a mouse and wishing to dispose of it in a humane way sought to drown it in a bucket of water. But the next day, upon removing the lid from the bucket, they found the little guy perched on tiptoe with his nose just barely above the water line. For the rest of the semester, I felt like that mouse—nearly drowning in a sea of responsibilities . . . and often blubbering, "I can't do this anymore!"

Though extra work, I found my lifeline through that Bible study. Just being around other Christian women and watching them surmount even greater struggles helped me to keep everything in perspective. Then too, we drew strength from each other and were constantly reminded to keep our eyes on Jesus.

By the power of the Holy Spirit, we who claim the name of Christ *can* stand on tiptoe for long periods of time. If you suffer from overload:

- Cry out to God. He loves you and cares about your every need.
- Draw strength and power from Jesus through the daily reading of His Word.
- Seek fellowship with other Christians. Though scarred, weathered, and crooked, they make great leaning posts.

For further reflection:
How did God help the great leader Moses, and Elijah the prophet when they were too weary to carry on? Read Exodus 17:8-15 and 1 Kings 19 respectively.

TRAGEDY

Do you not know that your body is a temple of the Holy Spirit, who is in you, whom you have received from God? You are not your own; you were bought at a price. Therefore honor God with your body (1 Corinthians 6:19-20).

No temptation has seized you except what is common to man. And God is faithful; he will not let you be tempted beyond what you can bear. But when you are tempted, he will also provide a way out so you can stand up under it (1 Corinthians 10:13).

Is any of one of you in trouble? He should pray . . . Is any one of you sick? He should call the elders of the church to pray over him and anoint him with oil in the name of the Lord (James 5:13-14).

Jake never made it to college. A week before his scheduled arrival at a state university, he committed suicide. His untimely death wreaked havoc on his rural community; Jake was the son of a well-liked and respected family. No one even dreamed that stress over the prospect of attending college would allegedly induce this bright, popular, young man to take his own life. His neighbors cried over such a needless tragedy.

I'm unfamiliar with the status of Jake's relationship with the Savior. But even those who's faith is widely known sometimes feel so overwhelmed by depression that they too, in a moment of weakness, choose death. Just a couple of years ago, the suicide of Vince Ebo rocked the contemporary Christian music industry and spawned a great debate over whether or not God forgives those who commit such a sin and the ultimate destiny of their souls. On the one hand, Jesus said the only unforgivable sin is blasphemy against the Holy Spirit (see Matthew 12:31). On the other hand, is unrepentant sin forgiven? If not, can one who no longer lives then repent of their disobedience?

Regardless of this continuing debate over the salvation of those who take their own lives, one thing remains perfectly clear: Christians are called to live a life free of sin. Therefore, the taking of a life through suicide should *never* be an option for believers. Instead, we must trust our cares to Him who cares for us.

Are you so overwhelmed by depression, oppression, and trouble that suicide seems to be the only way out? Please! I beg you to seek—now, this very moment—the help of your campus chaplain, a local pastor, or the suicide prevention hotline. God promises to provide a way out of your despair. And more often than not that way comes in the form of loving brothers and sisters who know how to walk you through this darkness and into the light again.

For further reflection:
What about assisted suicide? Read 2 Samuel 1:5-16 and 1 Peter 2:9.

BOYS TOWN NATIONAL HOTLINE
1-800-448-3000*

NATIONAL RUNAWAY SWITCHBOARD
(they take suicide calls as well)
1-800-621-4000*

During business hours you may obtain a referral from
AMERICAN ASSOCIATION OF SUICIDOLOGY
1-202-237-2280*

If you are in a crisis situation and don't have this book in hand, dial 911. The dispatcher can put you in touch with those who know how to help.

---

* The number was valid at the time this book was printed. There is no affiliation whatsoever between this organization and the author or publisher of this book. Likewise, neither the author or the publisher of this book are responsible for any advice given.

~~~

FAST FOOD

And we urge you brothers . . . be patient with everyone (1 Thessalonians 5:14).

But the fruit of the spirit is love, joy, peace, *patience,* kindness, goodness, faithfulness, gentleness and self-control (Galations 5:22).

A fool gives vent to his anger, but a wise man keeps himself under control (Proverbs 29:11).

Because I'd failed to bring my usual packed lunch and with time between classes running short, I sought to satisfy my growling stomach with a sandwich from the nearest fast food restaurant. I whizzed up to the drive-thru intercom, clipped out my order, and then hurriedly joined the line of waiting vehicles. However, instead of moving along towards the pickup window, this line of vehicles simply sat . . . and sat . . . and sat.

Ten minutes clicked by. With each passing second my frustration and anger mounted. "What in the world is going on up there?!" I shouted to myself. " I thought this was fast food?!" Being sandwiched in between two other cars made leaving impossible; I had no choice but to sit and stew. Finally reaching the window, I wasted no time in hurling off a well-deserved insult to the employee in-side. She calmly responded that the customer two cars ahead of me had seen fit to change her order three times. I grabbed my food and drove off in a huff.

Remorse quickly set in. How could I, a professing Christian, have acted like such a jerk?!

Patience is a fruit of the Holy Spirit that reigns within my heart. It is a gift given to me by Jesus Christ. However, unless I choose to make use of this gift, possessing it is of little or no value.

So, how does one go about making use of patience? The fol-lowing may lend some insight into this question:

- First, we must recognize that *we* are responsible for our own actions.
- *I* tried to squeeze too much activity into too short of a time span thereby setting *myself* up for frustration.
- Instead of sitting and stewing, we can use our idle moments to seek God's face. I could have used some of my time in the fast food lane to pray for an increase in patience, peace, and self-control.
- Praising God brings rest for the soul. Instead of wallowing in my frustration, I also could have taken some of those rare moments of inactivity to sing praises unto our Lord.

What about you? Do you foolishly vent your anger or wisely maintain self-control?

For further reflection:
For a greater understanding of the many facets of and warnings regarding patience read Proverbs 14:29, 15:18, 17:27, 19:19, and 22:24-25.

OPENING THE FLOODGATES

Be sure to set aside a tenth of all that your fields produce each year . . . so that you may learn to revere the Lord your God always . . . and so that the Lord your God may bless you in all the work of your hands (Deuteronomy 14:22, 23,29).

For if the willingness is there, the gift is acceptable according to what one has, not according to what he does not have (2 Corinthians 8:12).

"Bring the whole tithe into the storehouse, that there may be food in my house. Test me in this," says the Lord Almighty, "and see if I will not throw open the floodgates of heaven and pour out so much blessing that you will not have room enough for it" (Malachi 3:10).

My son, Jesse, returned home for summer break with dire financial straits looming on the horizon. Not only was he in debt to his father due to unexpected car repairs, but leaving for a summer with Teen Missions, International—in just four short weeks—made acquiring a steady paycheck both impractical and impossible. Therefore, he humbly resigned himself to discharging the repair debt through odd jobs and accepting an interlude of poverty.

One Saturday during this period, Jesse played a gig at the local coffeehouse. After the performance, a patron purchased one of Jesse's $6 cassettes with a ten dollar bill and told him to keep the change. Jesse put six dollars towards the tape's production costs and laid the other four dollars on his dresser. When I playfully commented about his rise from destitution, he responded, "Yes, now I finally have something to give to God."

We weren't able to attend church the next morning but true to his word, that four dollars stayed on Jesse's dresser until he deposited *all* of it in the offering plate the following week.

In the meantime, I visited a thrift shop and purchased Jesse some cheap work pants to be thrown away after the "boot camp" portion of his mission. Three days after giving that four dollars to God, while trying on a pair of those freshly laundered pants, Jesse reached into the pocket (which I *had* checked before laundering) and pulled out a neatly folded, washed and dried, ten dollar bill. Amazing! The Lord returned to Jesse more than double his gift to God!

Being in college and poor does not excuse us from tithing because tithing has nothing to do with money. Instead, placing a portion of our earnings in the offering plate is a direct expression of our heart attitude towards God.

So, how's your heart attitude been lately?

For further reflection:
Read what happened to Ananias and Sapphira when they lied about their tithe in Acts 5:1-11.

—*mm*—

CAN YOU SPARE A DIME?

The rich rule over the poor, and the borrower is servant to the lender (Proverbs 22:7).

Do not be a man who strikes hands in pledge or puts up security for debts; if you lack the means to pay, your very bed will be snatched from under you (Proverbs 22:26-27).

Let no debt remain outstanding, except the continuing debt to love one another (Romans 13:8).

Jesse planned to take his date ice skating at an off-campus rink. However, he needed to overcome one slight obstacle: transportation. Since his own car was unavailable at the time, Jesse smooth-talked his roommate, Mike, into letting him borrow his truck. (Which really belonged to Mike's brother who was working on a fishing vessel off the coast of Alaska.)

Undaunted by one of Pennsylvania's many snowstorms, Jesse and date set out for the big city. Traffic clipped along the interstate at a breathtaking 35mph. Suddenly, Jesse hit an ice patch, lost control of the truck, hit a guardrail, and moved into the path of an oncoming vehicle. The ensuing collision totaled his roommate's truck. Miraculously, the occupants of both vehicles walked away from the accident. Jesse, however, found it much more difficult to walk away from the trouble he'd caused his roommate. The insurance company's eventual cash settlement to Mike's brother and Jesse's monthly deductible payments did little to provide replacement transportation for Mike. Additionally, Mike's insurance rating bore the brunt of Jesse's mishap.

My friend, Susan, had completed all of the requirements for graduation but one—a cross cultural experience. Her university allowed students to "walk" during graduation exercises with the understanding that the cross cultural credit be satisfied the next semester. Susan registered for the cross cultural experience but didn't have enough money to cover the trip's costs. I agreed to loan her the deficit, she agreed to repay me in monthly installments, her graduation came off without a hitch, and she greatly enjoyed the trip abroad.

The first loan payment arrived on time; subsequent payments did not. I felt like a heel having to remind Susan of the debt and she felt bad about being tardy. She eventually made two double payments which allowed the debt to cancel out on time. However, we each lamented the strain this situation placed on our friendship.

While scripture does not prohibit borrowing, God does warn of its probable entrapment. Since Christians *must* repay their debts, they set themselves up for grave hardship when circumstances beyond their control interfere with that responsibility. In essence, by choosing to borrow, we may be selling ourselves into months of emotional and financial slavery.

Do you want to become a slave? Do you consider the cost when asking your roommate to spring for pizza and you'll pay him back later, or borrowing her CD, calculator, or car?

For further reflection:
If you borrow something and it breaks while in your possession, what must you do? Read Exodus 22:14-15.

~~~~~

A FLAME AT BOTH ENDS

Better one handful with tranquillity than two handfuls with toil and chasing after the wind (Ecclesiastes 4:6).

But Martha was distracted by all the preparations that had to be made (Luke 10:40).

Be still and know that I am God (Psalm 46:10).

Barely three weeks into the fall semester I ran into a fellow Mass Communication major at the local copy center. We chatted while standing in line, sharing news of our summer exploits and fall courses. I noted her weariness but was nonetheless surprised when she commented about being fatigued. "How can you be tired already?" I joked. "The semester's just begun!" She then recited her current activities: twenty semester hours; chairing a student organization; service sorority involvement; and development of a campus ministry affiliated with her denomination. No wonder she was dragging!

My son, Jesse, experienced a semester of overdoing as well. In addition to a full academic schedule and playing guitar in numerous performance practices and gigs, he was working over thirty hours a week as sound engineer for the School of Music. One night, while on duty at his campus job and ready to collapse, he phoned home. Trembling, he confessed that due to such a hectic schedule he'd not eaten in twenty-four hours. A delivered pizza solved the immediate problem. But only by the grace of God did he complete that semester without a nervous breakdown.

The human body's physical and mental stamina is not limitless; God designed us with the ability to accomplish only so much in a twenty-four hour period. (Perhaps to humble us?) Running on overload wrecks havoc on our physical well-being. It also distracts us from spending time with God. And such busyness ultimately amounts to little more than chasing after the wind. After all, *nothing* is more important than our relationship with Him.

Are you overdoing? What or whom have you been chasing lately?

For further reflection:
When man tried to establish his own greatness, how did God humble him? Read Genesis 11:1-9.

43

MAN'S WISDOM VS. GOD'S

Trust in the Lord with all your heart and lean not on your own
understanding; in all your ways acknowledge him and he will
make your paths straight (Proverbs 3:5-6).

Do not deceive yourselves. If any one of you thinks he is wise by
the standards of this age, he should become a "fool" so that he
may become wise. For the wisdom of this world is foolishness
in God's sight (1 Corinthians 3:18-19).

We do however, speak a message of wisdom among the mature,
but not the wisdom of this age or of the rulers of this age, who
are coming to nothing (1 Corinthians 2:6).

As I sat in class listening to the professor lecture on the five
ethical principles said to have merit, I wavered between being
appalled and amused. Of course moral relativism isn't new, but for
the first time in my life I was forced to pay attention to it. As the
Prof reiterated, "You need to decide which of these principles you
will live by so that when moral choices arise, you aren't confused,"
I thought, "What craziness. All these people really need is a good
dose of old-fashioned scripture memory work. Or maybe they
should just carry around one of those laminated cards with the

Ten Commandments printed on it!" Really, the whole scenario was quite ludicrous.

I came to college to gain understanding. But I must remember that there is a difference between man's understanding and God's. Man's wisdom remains limited to the finite—those things he can see, hear, and prove—knowledge which he often expands upon and changes. God's wisdom is omniscient and infinite—all knowing truth that never changes; it remains the same yesterday, today, and tomorrow.

Man has been jealous of God's wisdom and perverted His truth since the fall. " 'You will surely not die,' the serpent said to the woman. 'For God knows that when you eat of it your eyes will be opened, and you will be like God, knowing good and evil.' " (Genesis 3:4-5).

Satan has a field day on the campuses of our colleges and universities. Here, with man so puffed up by his own intellect, Satan has no problem leading him to think he can cross over into God's territory. Paul warns us of such folly in Galations 1:7-8, "Evidently some people are throwing you into confusion and are trying to pervert the gospel of Christ. But even if we or *an angel from heaven* should preach a gospel other than the one we preached to you, let him be eternally condemned."

Knowing the fickle heart of man, God gave us His unchanging Word through the Holy Bible and has protected its integrity through thousands of years and numerous translations.* Contained therein we find all of the ethics you and I will ever need.

Who do you listen to when it comes to moral truth?

For further reflection:
What did Jesus do to refute the folly of satan? Read Matthew 4:1-11 with Deuteronomy 8:3, Psalm 91:11-12, Deuteronomy 6:16, and Deuteronomy 6:13.

---

* This truth has been thoroughly explored in *Evidence that Demands a Verdict* by Josh McDowell.

—*mm*—

A MATTER OF CONVENIENCE?

The word of the Lord came to me, saying, "Before I formed you in the womb I knew you, before you were born I set you apart" (Jeremiah 1:4-5).

As soon as the sound of your greeting reached my ears, *the baby in my womb leaped for joy* (Luke 1:44 italics added).

We who are strong ought to bear with the failing of the weak and not to please ourselves (Romans 15:1).

Recently our nation reacted with shock and anger when two university students killed their newborn baby and then disposed of him in a trash receptacle. Frankly, I find their outrage pitiful. After all, what difference does it make if an individual terminates a baby's life outside or inside of the womb? Don't both terminations serve the same purpose—that of eliminating the need to care for and raise a child? "Well," say the abortion proponents, "it's not the same thing. A fetus isn't a baby."

Several years ago, due to my ignorance of the scriptures, I fell prey to this same, twisted, logic. When a teenage relative approached me about her out-of-wedlock pregnancy and a possible abortion, I told her that it was her body and she should *choose* the "option" she felt most comfortable with. She wound up aborting the child.

Some time later, God opened my eyes to the truth about abortion. In that moment, a deep, penetrating sadness washed over me. I repented of the part I played in that baby's death and fully received God's grace, mercy, and forgiveness. Forgiveness however, did not restore life to the child. I now live, daily, with wistful thoughts of who she or he might have been.

Satan often deludes us with his twisted lies. In order to shed some light on the abortion fallacy, I offer the following scriptural analysis:

In 2 Samuel 1:6-16 the enemy advanced upon Saul, the king. Fearing mutilation he attempted suicide. Maimed but not yet dead, he admonished a young Amalakite to finish him off. The young man complied. However, when the Amalakite reported to David how Saul had died, David rebuked the young man and had him executed for murder. We should all take to heart David's solemn words to the assassin which 2 Samuel 1:14 records as follows: "Why were you not afraid to lift your hand to destroy the Lord's anointed?"

When an enemy threatened Jerusalem, King Hezekiah cried, "This day is a day of distress and rebuke and disgrace, *as when children come to the point of birth and there is no strength to deliver them*" (2 Kings 19:3). If it was mournful for unborn children to die in Hezekiah's time, is it any less mournful for them to die in our day and age?

"My frame was not hidden from you when I was made in the secret place. When I was woven together in the depths of the earth, your eyes saw my unformed body. All the days ordained for me were written in your book before one of them came to be" (Psalm 139:15-16). How can anyone read this passage or Isaiah 49:1,5, Galations 1:15, or Luke 1:43-44 and say that life does not begin at conception (or before)?!

Finally, let me comment on the issue of choice. As referred to in Romans 15:1, Philippians 2:4-5, and numerous other verses, God calls Christians to put the welfare of others before themselves. In fact, Christ gave His very life that *we* might not die in our sins.

A nine month pregnancy (literally hundreds of loving, childless couples stand in line ready to adopt at the end of those nine months) pales in comparison to His selfless sacrifice.

When faced with the burden of the cross, Christ didn't give in to Satan and take the convenient way out; neither should we.

For further reflection:

What if you've already been involved in an abortion? Read the story of David and Bathsheba in 2 Samuel chapter 11 along with David's confession and God's forgiveness in Psalm 32.

OUT OF TUNE

Do not be mislead: "Bad company corrupts good character" (1
Corinthians 15:33).

Finally brothers, whatever is true, whatever is noble, whatever
is right, whatever is pure, whatever is lovely, whatever is admirable—if anything is excellent or praiseworthy—think about
such things (Philippians 4:8).

Turn away from godless chatter and the opposing ideas of what
is falsely called knowledge, which some have so professed and
in so doing have wandered from the faith (1 Timothy 6:20-21).

Have you ever caught yourself unintentionally humming a particular tune or phrase? Do you drum on your steering wheel
when a cool song plays on the car stereo? Do you devour every
morsel of available information on your favorite recording artist
or dress in such a way that others automatically associate you with
a particular style of music? e.g. punk, rock, country, etc. If so, then
you already know about the power of music.

Music serves as the virtual mainstay of every college student
I know. All of us have at least one stereo in our living quarters.

And I often see students on campus pouring over the latest record club catalog.

But, I often wonder if we ever stop to consider the messages feeding into our brains through this very powerful art form. Are the lyrics producing true, noble, pure, right, lovely, admirable, excellent, and praiseworthy thoughts? Or are we filling our minds with godless chatter that will at best, hamper our spiritual growth or at worst, eventually lead us away from the faith? Do our favorite recording artists and fellow devotees fall into the category of "bad company"? Or do they encourage us to pursue upstanding lives either through the lyrics they sing or by example?

Hmm. Some of my music suddenly lost its appeal. What about yours?

For further reflection:
How powerful can song really be? Read 2 Chronicles 20:20-30.

THE TRANSFER RIDDLE

Paul and his companions traveled throughout the region of Phrygia and Galatia, having been kept by the Holy Spirit from preaching the word in the province of Asia. When they came to the border of Mysia they tried to enter Bithynia, but the Spirit of Jesus would not allow them to (Acts 16:6-7).

After Paul had seen the vision, we got ready at once to leave for Macedonia, concluding that God had called us to preach the gospel to them (Acts 16:10).

When we heard this, we and the people there pleaded with Paul not to go up to Jerusalem. Then Paul answered, "Why are you weeping and breaking my heart? I am ready not only to be bound, but also to die in Jerusalem for the name of the Lord Jesus." When he would not be dissuaded, we gave up and said, "the Lord's will be done" (Acts 21:12-14).

Despite my son, Jesse's, subconscious attempt to "create" a Music Business major, (he majored in Music his freshman year and Business Management his sophomore year) courses such as Copyright Law and Music Publishing just weren't available at his college. Additional concerns such as rising tuition, internship opportunities, and extracurricular opportunities led both student and parents to toss around the idea of transferring.

Advantages and disadvantages were considered. These included location, course offerings, internships, performance opportunities, transfer of credits, tuition/transportation costs, and friendships.

Since Jesse intended to pursue a career in contemporary Christian music, he felt a strong desire to attend a college in or near Nashville, TN. We soon learned that one of the finest Music Business programs in the nation hailed from Belmont University, located just blocks from downtown Nashville. Discovering that Belmont's strategic location enabled it to offer year round internships, that performance opportunities both on and off campus abound, and that the university's tuition rates suited our pocketbook, made the idea of transferring all the more enticing.

Not enticing was the prospect of losing several credits. Most colleges refuse to transfer credits for course work not corresponding with classes offered at their particular institution, or in which the student received a less than satisfactory grade report. Jesse's failure to apply himself during his first semester of college cost him dearly during transcript evaluation. (The loss of those credits eventually forced him to spend a summer taking classes.) Other disadvantages included the nine hour drive home from Nashville as opposed to the current two hour drive, and leaving behind several close friends.

Despite the logistical attributes or lack thereof, the ultimate question became, "Is the Holy Spirit prodding Jesse to make this move or are his desires based entirely on human whim?" God had *clearly* opened the doors for him to attend his first school. We needed to know that He was now *clearly* sending him elsewhere.

In the end, our doubts melted away, and God's purposes prevailed. It wasn't mere coincidence that the one college in Nashville which interested Jesse turned out to be a conservative Christian college. Nor was it coincidence that one of *my* professors in Virginia sang nothing but praises for this small school some 600 miles away. And when Jesse put forth the fleece of application, Belmont readily accepted him as a student into the Music Business program while turning others away.

If you are contemplating a transfer, carefully consider the options. You might want to make two columns on a sheet of paper, then list each advantage and disadvantage. In 2 Kings 19:14-19 we see that when King Hezekiah of Judah received a disturbing letter, he went to the temple, spread the letter before God, and prayed about the situation at hand. Lay your list before God and seek His face on the matter. Ask God to open doors that lead to His will for your life and close those which don't. He *will* direct your path.

For further reflection:
Read God's recorded tribute of Hezekiah in 2 Kings 18:5-7.

PROFESSOR WHO?

Let us therefore make every effort to do what leads to peace and to mutual edification (Romans 14:19).

All who are under the yoke of slavery should consider their masters worthy of full respect, so that God's name and our teaching may not be slandered (1 Timothy 6:1).

If your brother sins against you, go and show him his fault, just between the two of you. If he listens to you, you have won your brother over. But if he will not listen, take one or two others along, so that 'every matter may be established by the testimony of two witnesses.' If he refuses to listen to them, tell it to the church (Matthew 18:15-17).

Fall semester, first day of class. Dr. Highstone walked into the classroom, heaved a huge stack of paperwork onto the desk, introduced himself, and smugly commented, "Now everyone will run for the door." He then proceeded to spout off a list of "Highstone pet peeves" including drinks, food, hats, and tape recorders—all of which were prohibited in his classes. I sat through the rest of his boring lecture and attempted to take notes from his illegible handwriting. The next day I went to the registrar and dropped the class;

without the privilege of using a tape recorder, if I began to flounder (Dr. Highstone left no doubt as to the course's difficulty) my GPA would be doomed.

Jenny, a conservative Christian at another college, found herself in complete disagreement with her professor on most of the issues raised during class discussions. This made for a rather strained teacher-student relationship. At semester's end, students were required to write an extensive research paper. Jenny crafted a well written essay but failed to properly cite her footnotes. Seizing upon this oversight, the professor wrongly accused her of plagiarism, totally slammed her self-esteem, threatened to report her for cheating, and demanded she rewrite the entire paper immediately—despite the fact that she had other exams to prepare for.

A string of impressive, academic credentials on a professor's resume does not guarantee that he or she is a good educator and certainly lends no insight into his or her personality. Therefore, it's a good bet that at some point during our college experience, we'll come into contact with one of these undesirables.

Avoiding insolent, boring, or culpable professors is our first avenue towards making every effort to live in peace. When that avenue is blocked (a must have class and he/she is the only available instructor) we can ascribe to the process Christ laid down for situations involving persons who have committed an offense: talking to the professor about our concerns, going to the professor with other class members about concerns, and meeting with the dean or college president about our concerns. But irregardless of the eventual outcome of these efforts, we still owe the professor—by virtue of his/her authority—undue respect.

As Christians, even the way we respond to unpleasant situations or persons serves as a witness—good or bad—for Jesus Christ. What kind of witness have you been lately?

For further reflection:
How must we respond to our enemies? Read Matthew 5:43-48.

WISE AS SERPENTS

Therefore be as shrewd as snakes and as innocent as doves (Matthew 10:16).

A simple man believes anything but a prudent man gives thought to his steps (Proverbs 14:15).

It is not good to have zeal without knowledge, nor to be hasty and miss the way (Proverbs 19:2).

James Madison University has a very sophisticated title for students like myself: "nontraditional"; it's a nice way of saying, "older". Well, having gone around the block a few times makes me not only older but also wiser. Right? Not always!

This past Saturday I went to the city with my Navy son, Jamie, to help him purchase a car. After a full day of shopping around we at last found the Jeep of his dreams: a 1993 Wrangler with only 10,000 miles on it. We filled out papers . . . and waited. We haggled . . . and waited. After two hours we were ready to sign on the dotted line. Since the sticker failed to mention it, I made a point to inquire about the balance of the factory warranty. The sales associate assured me that on Monday morning I need only call a Jeep or Chrysler dealer (we were purchasing from a Buick dealer) and ask to have the warranty transferred. However, on Monday morning, the sky started falling. According to the "powers that be", the Jeep of his dreams had been totaled and rebuilt; there was no warranty.

Aside from the fact that my next long distance phone bill will be much higher, nearly 500 miles were added to my vehicle, I spent $75 for gas, motel, and food, and lost two days of precious writing time—everything turned out okay. Jamie brought the Jeep back from Norfolk, we returned it to the dealer (they claimed ignorance but gave us little hassle), and I returned Jamie to duty in Norfolk.

We live in a big bad world where integrity is indeed rare. Through His Word, God offers divine wisdom on how to deal with this societal shortcoming. Heeding that wisdom as a lamp unto our feet will go a long way in preventing you and I from stubbing our toes.

The entire time we were signing that contract, I kept thinking, "We're rushing things. There are too many unknowns." But, Jamie needed to be back on base by Monday morning and wanted to drive there himself, so . . .

Gaining God's wisdom requires not only hiding His Word in our hearts but putting it into practice as well. Are you reading and heeding God's wisdom?

For further reflection:
Though Solomon was wise in many ways, he foolishly failed to heed God's warnings and commands. Read what his folly cost the nation of Israel in 1 Kings 11:1-13.

~~~~

QUICKSAND

Flee from sexual immorality. All other sins a man commits are outside his body, but he who sins sexually sins against his own body (1 Corinthians 6:18).

You have heard that it was said, 'Do not commit adultery'. But I tell you that anyone who looks at a woman lustfully has already committed adultery with her in his heart. If your right eye causes you to sin, gouge it out and throw it away. It is better for you to lose one part of your body than for your whole body to be thrown into hell (Matthew 5:27-29).

Finally brothers, whatever is true, whatever is noble, whatever is right, whatever is pure, whatever is lovely, whatever is admirable—if anything is excellent or praiseworthy—think about such things (Philippians 4:8).

In 1989 the state of Florida executed Ted Bundy for the murder of a college coed. All totaled, he sexually assaulted and brutally killed at least thirty-five women. When envisioning the kind of man Ted Bundy must have been, one pictures a lecherous, disgusting, criminal type individual who obviously grew up on the wrong side of the tracks. Nothing could be farther from the truth.

Instead, Mr. Bundy was a handsome, well-educated, young man who grew up in a typical, God-fearing, middle income family. So, whatever possessed this all-American, boy-next-door to commit such heinous crimes?

According to his final interview, recorded just hours before execution, Mr. Bundy admitted that he, and the women he murdered, were all victims of pornography. This intelligent, broken man, spoke candidly of a progressive addiction which eventually desensitized him to all but the most brutal forms of sex—those involving sexual deviance and murder.

In 1984 Dr. Dolf Zillman presented evidence, from a study he'd performed, which strongly suggested that repeated exposure to pornography produced boredom towards normal sexual behavior, an increased appetite for more bizarre sexual materials, and a trivialization of rape.* Additional studies have not only confirmed these findings but gone on to suggest a distinct correlation between pornography and broken families, child molestation, sexual assault, and rape.†

Despite overwhelming evidence regarding pornography's ravages upon society, the industry continues to grow and thrive. And with the advent of the internet, people who pander this filth have found an easy way to get their destructive material into the homes of every computer oriented family . . . and into the minds of every college student with on-line access.

Just a few weeks ago, I learned, through a rather surprising turn of events, of the pornography addiction of two college age men—both professing Christians. "How can this be?" I cried. "How can two committed Christians get themselves wrapped up in such sin?!"

The ultimate answer comes in not eating enough spiritual food and thus succumbing to spiritual weakness. But, the immediate answer can be found in the old adage, "Curiosity killed the cat."

Men and women, hear me loud and clear—visiting porno sites on the internet is no lark! Pornography drowns its victims like quicksand. You don't see this sucking evil until you've innocently fallen into the pool and once there you just keep on sinking.

Fortunately for these two young men, they have a caring friend who's helping them break free from this addiction. If you or someone you know has fallen into this same pool of quicksand, I beg you to get help. Call the National Coalition for the Protection of Children and Families at 513-521-6227 or log onto their website at <www.nationalcoalition.org>. They have the resources to assist you in digging out of this victimizing pit.

For further reflection:
Paul once spoke about his struggle with wanting to do good but continuing to do evil. He eventually exclaimed, "What a wretched man I am! Who will rescue me from this body of death? Thanks be to God—through Jesus Christ our Lord!" For the full account, read Romans 7:14-25.

---

* Dr. Jerry Kirk. *The Mind Polluters*. Thomas Nelson Publishers. 1985.
† Attorney General's Commission on Pornography, Final Report, July 7, 1986.

DESENSITIZED

You were running a good race. Who cut in on you and kept you from obeying the truth? (Galations 5:7).

He said to them, "You are the ones who justify yourselves in the eyes of men, but God knows your hearts. What is highly valued among men is detestable in God's sight" (Luke 16:15).

You must no longer live as the gentiles—who are darkened in their understanding and separated from the life of God because of the ignorance that is in them due to the hardening of their hearts. *Having lost all sensitivity*, they indulge in every kind of impurity, with a continual lust for more (Ephesians 4:17-19 paraphrased).

It's hard to live side by side with the world and remain unpolluted by their standards. Christians don't murder those who cut in line at the movie theater. However, do we cheer the screen actor who shoots an annoying surplus store proprietor? Most Christians live as law abiding citizens. However, do we purposefully drive above the posted speed limits? Christians don't rob banks. However, do we "take" souvenir salt shakers from restaurants or bath towels from motels? Christians don't regularly use the "F" word. However, do we speak the Lord's name in vain?

Eroding values lead to eroding faith and Satan masterfully uses this truism to his benefit. By subtly desensitizing us through worldly philosophies, he tempts us to compromise our values and thus cross the border from God's camp into his.

Banking institutions teach their tellers to recognize counterfeit money by studying real currency. Christians can only avoid desensitization by studying God's Word and hiding it in our hearts.

Is Satan luring you into compromising your values? When was the last time you read the Bible?

For further reflection:
Does Satan use only the "outside world" to desensitize us to sin? Read 2 Timothy 4:3-4.

—*mm*—

LOVES ME. LOVES ME NOT.

Love is patient, love is kind. It does not envy, it does not boast, it is not proud. It is not rude, it is not self-seeking, it is not easily angered, it keeps no record of wrongs. It always protects, always trusts, always hopes, always perseveres (1 Corinthians 13:4,5,7).

However, each one of you also must love his wife as he loves himself, and the wife must respect her husband (Ephesians 5:33).

Wives, submit to your husbands, as is fitting in the Lord. Husbands, love your wives and do not be bitter with them (Colossians 3:18-19, KJV).

Heather surprised me and my college friends by coming home from a mission trip and announcing her engagement to a Canadian she'd met while in Haiti; we all expected she and a local boyfriend to tie the knot.

My son, Jesse, and I dropped Jeff off in Roanoke on our way to Nashville. Jeff wanted to visit a girl he'd been corresponding with for over a year but had seen only twice. When we returned to pick him up, Jeff floated on cloud nine . . . within minutes we learned of his marriage engagement!

Many of you will marry or get engaged while attending college. Even at this very moment, some are contemplating wedlock.

Though surrounded by romance, marriage is a lifelong commitment that you should approach with your head as well as in response to your heart. As a matter of fact, if your head does not agree with your heart then *do not* take the gamble; the stakes will be burdensome.

The above scriptures represent God's blueprint for love that will last a lifetime. The following is my practical, experiential analysis:

- Love is patient—true love *puts up with* another's shortcomings, again and again and again.
- Love is kind—true love *goes out of its way* to comfort or encourage.
- Love does not envy—true love allows for *other* friendships, hobbies, interests, etc.
- Love does not boast—true love *is not* just for show.
- Love is not proud—true love does not *"lord it over"* another.
- Love is not rude—true love is *polite and gentle.*
- Love is not self-seeking—true love *cares more for* the other person *than for self.*
- Love is not easily angered—true love *overlooks* petty grievances.
- Love keeps no record of wrongs—true love *does not throw one's faults* or past mistakes *into his/her face.*
- Love always protects—true love *protects* the other's reputation, health, and life.
- Love always trusts—true love is not *suspicious* and does not *suffocate* the other individual.
- Love always hopes—true love is *confident* in self, spouse, and the relationship.
- Love always perseveres—true love is *in for the long haul* . . . for better *or worse,* till death do us part.
- True love recognizes that, for the sake of the union, compromises *must be* found.

For further reflection:
For several examples of true love read Ruth chapters 1 through 4.

52

SINGLES ANYONE?

For some are eunuchs because they were born that way; others were made that way by men; and others have renounced marriage because of the kingdom of heaven. The one who can accept this should accept it (Matthew 19:12).

Now to the unmarried and the widows I say: It is good for them to stay unmarried, as I am. But each man has his own gift from God; one has this gift, another has that (1 Corinthians 7:8-7).

I would like you to be free from concern. An unmarried man is concerned about the Lord's affairs—how he can please the Lord. But a married man is concerned about the affairs of this world—how he can please his wife—and his interests are divided. The same is true for an unmarried woman or virgin (1 Corinthians 7:32-34 paraphrased).

At age sixteen, Jesse heard God calling him into music ministry. While the Father has seen fit to delay how that ministry will work out, Jesse approaches his studies and extracurricular activities with the calling in mind.

Jesse also happens to be a very handsome young man with a winning personality and never lacking for a date. But recently, because of the call to ministry, he's wondered if God might also be asking him to remain single.

The truth from God's Word says that it's okay not to marry and indeed, preferable for some. For while a married man or woman *must* divide his/her time, money, and energy between God, spouse, and children, unmarried persons *can more freely* devote their resources to the cause of Christ.

Quite often we who are married, engaged, or going steady place undue pressure upon our single family members and friends. Certainly, many of these individuals do intend, one day, to enter into a marriage covenant and in God's *perfect timing* we can expect to witness such a blessed event. However, we must bear in mind that others may choose to stay single (even if for only a season) and we should rejoice with them in this decision.

Whether or not our Father intends for Jesse to stay unmarried remains a mystery. In the meantime, he's content to flirt a little, date a little, and wait upon God.

Whatever your marital status, present or future, may you live a life worthy of the Lord and please Him in every way (see Colossians 1:10).

For further reflection:
To marry or not to marry? God's litmus test is given in 1 Corinthians 7:9.

53

SEVENTY TIMES SEVEN

Then Peter came to Jesus and asked, "Lord, how many times shall I forgive my brother when he sins against me? Up to seven times?" Jesus answered, "I tell you, not seven times, but seventy-seven times" (Matthew 18:21-22).

For if you forgive men when they sin against you, your heavenly Father will also forgive you. But if you do not forgive men their sins, your Father will not forgive your sins (Matthew 6:14-15).

Be kind and compassionate to one another, forgiving each other, just as in Christ God forgave you (Ephesians 4:32).

Anger mounted with each passing moment. This was the second project meeting in which Karen had come to the table with nothing to show for a week's worth of research. Since our deadline loomed just over the horizon, Karen needed to get her act together in a real hurry; it just wasn't fair for someone else to do her research as well as their own. I left the meeting thoroughly annoyed.

The following week she presented the fruits of her labor—a pitiable amount of nothing which added precious little to the project. At meeting's end I angrily headed for the library.

We finished the assignment on time—no thanks to Karen. I couldn't wait to fill out the group member review sheets; I planned to include some pretty scathing remarks about this freeloading student. However, once the deserved criticism stared up at me in black and white, remorse set in; I tore up the sheet and wrote a new one.

I'd really rather not forgive many of the offenses done to me by others; especially those which cause deep, abiding pain. But God declares that if I refuse to forgive men when they sin against me, then He will not forgive my sin. Ouch! That hurts!

With lots of determination and conversation with God, I eventually gave up my anger towards Karen. How about you? Are you harboring bitterness against someone? Do you want the benefits of God's grace and mercy? Then let go of unforgiveness; you'll be glad you did.

For further reflection:
Does unforgiveness relate to unanswered prayer? Read Mark 11:24-25.

—*mm*—

STAYING ONLINE

Then Jesus told his disciples a parable to show them that they should always pray and not give up (Luke 18:1).

Be joyful in hope, patient in affliction and faithful in prayer (Romans 12:12).

And pray in the Spirit on all occasions with all kinds of prayers and requests (Ephesians 6:18).

The work required just to stay afloat in many of my classes was so demanding. No matter how organized my intentions, assigned reading always lagged behind my handy dandy schedule. This time crunch took its toll on my devotions and prayer life. But after seeing my Christlike attitude slip down the drain, I grew very disciplined in, at least, keeping up with daily Bible study. Yet, a balanced spiritual diet requires more than scripture alone; it wasn't long before I truly craved that intimate time of prayer.

God makes no secret of the fact that a deep, abiding relationship with Him constitutes the marrow of our sustenance. And relationships must be nurtured. Were we to stop spending time with our friends, they would eventually become more like acquaintances rather than bosom buddies. Prayer serves as the avenue through which we spend time with God.

There are various ways of maintaining a meaningful prayer life. Jesus went outdoors to a solitary place; King David wrote his prayers in a journal (we know it as the Psalms); Daniel prayed on his knees. All bowed before the Creator in complete humility and adoration . . . on a regular basis.

I wish I could say that my prayer life is now in order. It isn't. Satan knows how much power there is in coming before God and he relentlessly does all that he can to keep me and my Lord apart. But as I continue to grow in Christ, so does my resistance to the devil's schemes.

Are you spending time with God on a regular basis?

For further reflection:
Read what Jesus prayed—specifically for you and me—in John 17:20-26.

—*mm*—

THE JUNIOR SLUMP

Not that I have already obtained all this, or have already been made perfect, but I press on to take hold of that for which Christ Jesus took hold of me (Philippians 3:12).

Therefore, since we are surrounded by such a cloud of witnesses, let us throw off everything that hinders and the sin that so easily entangles, and let us run with perseverance the race marked out for us. Let us fix our eyes on Jesus, the author and perfecter of our faith (Hebrews 12:1-2).

You were running a good race. Who cut in on you and kept you from obeying the truth? That kind of persuasion does not come from the one who calls you (Galatians 5:7-8).

Nearly every student I know has encountered the "junior slump". After five or six semesters of constantly pushing our intellectual limits we feel as though we just can't go on. We're mentally exhausted and emotionally ready for a change of pace.*

Towards the end of his junior year Jesse began to hint around about dropping out of school; he was tired of the college grind and wanted to "get on with life." Iron clad opposition from the homefront cooled his desires for the next semester but by the middle of his senior year, the restlessness had escalated to a point of frenzy. Just ending the fifth semester myself, I could relate perfectly well to his slump. However, we all feared that were he to pull out, even for a semester break, he'd likely never return and the tens of thousands of dollars invested in that "elusive piece of paper" would be for naught. In stepped God.

God really does care about us and promises that when tempted beyond what we can bear, He provides a godly way for us to handle the temptation (see 1 Corinthians 10:13). Out of the blue, our loving Father opened the doors for Jesse to join a Christian rock band, spend a semester touring the country, and receive internship credit for the experience. Not only did this provide the break he so desperately needed but the internship credit allowed him to keep his student status. At the end of the tour he returned to classes still anxious to "get on with life" but with a renewed commitment to "finish the race".

I hesitate to say that no one should leave school early. Sometimes God clearly calls us away. However, our education is a great investment in time, money, and God's purpose for our life. (Hopefully we sought God's will before enrolling in college!) It would be foolish to throw in the towel without a great deal of prayer and careful consideration.

If you find yourself fighting restlessness, look to the Savior. His answer might be as simple as a changed attitude or as involved as an internship. But whatever way He chooses, rest assured, it's the course marked out for *you*.

For further reflection:
What's the ultimate prize for which we all press forward? Read 1 Corinthians 9:24-25 and 2 Timothy 4:8.

---

* A business owner once told me that his company only employs college graduates because a degree indicates that an individual is (a) trainable and (b) someone who perseveres.

COMING OUT OF THE CLOSET

The Lord God said, "It is not good for the man to be alone. I will make a helper suitable for him." Now the Lord God had formed out of the ground all the beasts of the field and all the birds of the air . . . But for Adam no suitable helper was found . . . Then the Lord God made a woman from the rib he had taken out of the man, and he brought her to the man . . . For this reason a man will leave his father and mother and be united to his wife, and they will become one flesh (Genesis 2:18-24).

Because of this, God gave them over to shameful lusts. Even their women exchanged natural relations for unnatural ones. In the same way the men also abandoned natural relations with women and were inflamed with lust for one another. Men committed indecent acts with other men, and received in themselves the due penalty for their perversion. Furthermore, since they did not think it worthwhile to retain the knowledge of God, he gave them over to a depraved mind, to do what ought not to be done (Romans 1:26-28).

But since there is so much immorality, each man should have his own wife, and each woman her own husband. The husband should fulfill his marital duty to his wife, and likewise the wife to her husband (1 Corinthians 7:2-3).

I really liked Tracy. We met in microeconomics class and became friends when he agreed to help me with some difficult econ homework. Despite busy schedules, we sometimes lingered after our studies to discuss other topics of interest. When the next semester found us tracking the same courses, we occasionally stopped to chat either before or after class. I knew God was using me to witness to this young man but I never expected that when Tracy finally broached the subject of faith, I'd be called upon to address the issue of homosexuality. "God, couldn't you give me a more benign subject like 'why do I need a Savior'?!"

Tracy asked some pretty pointed questions; he didn't believe homosexuality to be sin. I did the best I could off of the top of my head and promised to return to the next class session with scriptures. I then spent the next two days pouring over the Bible.

My research yielded the following: God placed Adam in a beautiful garden which lacked no good thing. Lush vegetation, flowing rivers, a variety of animal life, and fellowship with God all abounded in the garden. Still, Adam felt the void of a suitable helpmate. Why did Adam feel a void? Because of all creation, only man was made in the image of God . . . but only half the image and thus the void. So God created woman . . . who embodied the other half of God's image. Together, they, with their different yet complimentary physiological and psychological characteristics, represent the complete personality of the creator (see endnote and Genesis 1:27). A sexual union between the male and female sealed the marriage of these two parts to create the whole.

This marriage can be likened to a two piece puzzle with each piece designed to fit perfectly together thus forming a beautiful picture of God (as well as Christ and the church, see Ephesians 5:22-32). Since one male puzzle piece can never be perfectly joined to another male puzzle piece—no matter how effeminate—any attempt to emulate marital oneness (i.e. engage in sexual activity) creates a distorted picture and is an abomination to God. (The same holds true for females.)

God reiterates this point throughout scripture. Passages you may want to investigate include: Leviticus 18:22; Mark 7:20-23; Romans 6:11-14; 1 Corinthians 6: 9-10; Hebrews 13:4; and Jude 7.

Sadly, after I presented Tracy with solid Biblical evidence that homosexuality was indeed a sin, he stopped pausing to chat after class. (Coincidence?) I tried, via Email, to create some spiritual dialog but to no avail. Now, the only avenue remaining open is prayer.

For further reflection:
Can those born with a "bent" towards homosexuality or those currently involved in such a lifestyle be regenerated? Read Psalm 51:5-7 and 1 Corinthians 6:9-11 paying particular attention to verse 11.

ENDNOTE: *Being created in someone's image does not imply that the creation is an exact duplicate of the creator. "Man" is not God. Your image can be embodied in a life-sized photo of yourself but that photo certainly isn't you.*

‑‑‑*‑‑*‑‑*‑‑

READY CASH

Suppose a brother or sister is without clothes and daily food. If one of you says to him, "Go, I wish you well; keep warm and well fed," but does nothing about his physical needs, what good is it? (James 2:15–16).

Do not take advantage of a widow or an orphan. If you lend money to one of my people among you who is needy, do not be like a moneylender; charge him no interest (Exodus 22:22,25).

My command is this: Love each other as I have loved you. Greater love has no one than this, that he lay down his life for his friends (John 15:12-13).

In order to alleviate their bleak financial status, Peter and a group of his friends decided to pay a visit to the local plasma center. The going rate per pint seemed a fair deal so they all lined up at the counter. Protocol called for an initial finger prick whereby a small sample of blood was gathered for testing; only "clean" blood qualified for purchase. When his turn came, Peter stood nonchalantly before the technician and flinched only a little when the needle jabbed his finger. However, as the blood began to ooze, Peter and all of his 6'1" frame fell straight back in a dead faint.

The impact of his head upon the concrete floor resulted in a trip to the emergency room, nine stitches, whiplash, and some minor, reoccurring neurological problems.

Nowhere in scripture does it say, "Thou shalt not *sell* thy blood; it shall be *donated* to those in need." And, this devotional is not intended to address the doctrinal issue of whether or not the donating of blood is acceptable to God. The issue at hand is the greedy profiteering from those things which ought to be freely given, not sold.

Is it right to sell babies to barren couples who so desperately want a child? Is it right to sell humanitarian assistance to helpless victims of earthquakes, floods, tornadoes, and hurricanes? Is it right to sell the message of eternal life? Is it right to sell the "gift of life"? God calls Christians to love one another. Profiteering from someone else's helplessness is not love.

I do not believe that God struck Peter down because he intended to make a profit from his blood. In fact, the Emergency Medical Technicians who responded to the accident claimed it was a miracle he survived such a blow to the head. However, God did use this incident to provoke some serious thought about right and wrong ways to make money.

Are you in the habit of taking advantage of the helpless and the needy?

For further reflection:
What did Nehemiah say to those who were profiting from a famine? Read Nehemiah 5:1-13.

APARTMENT VS. DORM

My son, preserve sound judgment and discernment, do not let them out of your sight; they will be life for you, an ornament to grace your neck. Then you will go your way in safety, and your foot will not stumble; . . . when you lie down, your sleep will be sweet (Proverbs 3:21-24).

It is not good to have zeal without knowledge, nor to be hasty and miss the way (Proverbs 19:2).

So Paul and Barnabas were appointed, along with some other believers, to go up to Jerusalem to see the apostles and elders about this question . . . The apostles and elders met to consider this question (Acts 15:2,6).

Halfway into his junior year, our son, Jesse, grew disenchanted with dorm life and sought the "greener pastures" of apartment living. Lured by prospects of greater privacy, kitchen privileges, and cheaper rent, and assured by Jesse of the Christian character of each roommate, we gave our blessing upon the move.

My husband and I married young. In so doing we never experienced apartment life with roommates and therefore had no clue as to the possible pitfalls of such a living arrangement. Too bad—

we might have saved our son months of heartache. Not only did two of his three roommates turn out to be extremely inconsiderate in terms of cleanliness, overnight guests, television usage, and failure to pay for groceries, at the end of the lease period they left Jesse with $300 worth of unpaid electric and telephone bills. (Both accounts were in his name.)

After watching Jesse go through three subsequent apartment/house/roommate experiences and hearing tales from other college students I offer the following words of wisdom regarding the move from dorm to apartment:

First, carefully consider the advantages of dorm living verses those of apartment living.

<u>Dorm Advantages</u>	<u>Apartment Advantages</u>
• Easier to make friends.	• More freedom.
• More in tune with campus activities	• Cheaper rent (possibly).
• More privacy.	• Eat what you want when you want.
• Not responsible for roommate's debts.	• Larger living space.
• Not locked into a lease.	• Parents need not stay in motel when they visit.
• Meals prepared by someone else.	• Can remain in apartment during school breaks when dorms are normally closed.
• Don't need own furniture or housewares.	
• Limited housekeeping responsibilities.	
• No need to worry about getting to class if auto breaks down or associated expenses.	

Once you've decided to try apartment life, consider the following:

• How many roommates will you have to share a bathroom with? Or a bedroom with?

134

- What about the lifestyles of those with whom you plan to room? Are they neat freaks or slobs? Couch potatoes or television haters? Are their lifestyles compatible with yours?
- Is *each roommate* equally and legally responsible for the lease?
- Will each roommate have his/her own toll call restricted telephone that he/she is financially responsible for? (Toll call restriction requires the entering of a private code to access long distance dialing.)
- If not, then will you ask the phone company to put a block put on all toll calls and have everyone use prepaid calling cards for long distance dialing? Or is someone willing to be the fall guy if another roommate racks up a hefty long distance bill he or she can't or won't pay?
- Who pays for the electric, cable, water, and trash pick-up? How will you insure that each person pays their fair share?
- What about groceries?

- What about housekeeping chores? Dirty houses attract insects, rodents, and germs.
- How about dinner and overnight guests? How many nights in a row can a friend stay for dinner and sleep on the sofa without paying for food, hot water, electric, etc.?
- What will be the consequences for roommates who fail to meet financial obligations?
- How will you resolve differences? (A monthly pow wow might help.)
- Who sees to it that the checks for rent and utilities are written, put in stamped envelopes, and actually mailed? (Once again, a monthly pow wow can help solve this problem.)

Finally, remember to seek God's will in deciding where you should live. Only *He* sees the big picture.

For further reflection:
Read the riveting account of Jesus accepting to the Father's will in Mark 14:32-36 and Luke 22:39-42.

———

BEAUTY OR BEAST

Like a gold ring in a pig's snout is a beautiful woman who shows no discretion (Proverbs 11:22).

Charm is deceptive, and beauty is fleeting; but a woman who fears the Lord is to be praised (Proverbs 31:30).

Your beauty should not come from outward adornment, such as braided hair and the wearing of gold jewelry and fine clothes. Instead, it should be that of your inner self, the unfading beauty of a gentle and quiet spirit, which is of great worth in God's sight (1 Peter 3:3).

Ever since my thirtieth birthday, I've worn my hair shoulder-length and with bangs. A few weeks ago, a shag type hairstyle modeled in a magazine caught my attention. After mustering up the courage, and with a photo of the desired style in hand, I took the plunge and entered a beauty shop. When I left, my hair looked nothing like that model's.

My daughter, Elizabeth, made polite remarks about the cut and out of sympathy spent an hour trying to do something (anything!) to make my hair look better. In the end we decided it "wasn't that bad" and "it will grow back". All that night I plotted how to disappear for a few weeks but ultimately decided I'd just have to face the music.

Nearly a week has passed. A few students in my classes did a double take but I've received no disgusting stares. My husband likes the haircut and a couple of Elizabeth's friends like it. Looking in the mirror is no longer a shock and, as Mark Lowry says, "This too shall pass."

While there is nothing wrong with wanting to look our best, Christians must remember that true beauty is found on the inside, not the outside. Spending an inordinate amount of energy and time worrying and chasing after outward beauty will not advance the Gospel of Christ. Cultivating and allowing His beauty to shine through us, will. No matter how my hair is styled, can others still see the light of Christ in my eyes?

How about you? Are you obsessed with external appearances?

For further reflection:
For what purpose should we want to look our best? Read 2 Samuel 12:20, Genesis 41:14-16, and the book of Esther.

OBSTACLE COURSE

"For I know the plans I have for you," declares the Lord, "plans to prosper you and not to harm you, plans to give you hope and a future" (Jeremiah 29:11).

Surely it was for my benefit that I suffered such anguish. In Your love You kept me (Isaiah 38:17).

And we know that in all things God works for the good of those who love Him and who have been called according to his purpose (Romans 8:28).

After visiting several prospective colleges, Jesse set his sights on a state university which offered a Music Industry degree. Each day he anxiously awaited the letter which would confirm his acceptance into that coveted institution. However, when written communication finally arrived, it read, "Dear Jesse, we regret . . ." Sorely disappointed, he battled weeks of depression.

In the midst of this depression and much to his surprise, Jesse received a generous offer of financial assistance from his second school of choice. Up to this point, any hope of funding an education at this private institution had been bleak indeed. However,

God is in the business of accomplishing His will and turned Jesse's fledgling hope into reality.

Attending this college gave Jesse numerous opportunities to hone his performance and songwriting skills—opportunities likely unavailable at the state university he sought to attend. Additionally, Jesse served as concert committee cochairman, and worked as a DJ at the college radio station. Each of these "learning experiences" proved invaluable when he transferred to Belmont University. Within two months of that move, he landed his first non-college gig and continues to perform regularly.

Are you suffering from disappointment or even tragedy? Perhaps you can't find a ride home for fall break. Maybe you lost your campus job due to false accusations of theft. Even worse, perhaps someone violated you through the horror of date rape.

When such things occur, look to the One who keeps you in His love and works all things together for your good. Great and mighty are His plans for your life. If you continue to lean on Him, He *will* bring those plans to pass . . . regardless of the obstacles Satan throws your way.

For further reflection:
Why does God allow Christians to suffer? Read Romans 5:3-5, James 1:2-4 and James 1:12.

—*mm*—

DISLOCATED LANGUAGE

But now you must rid yourselves of all such things as these: anger, rage, malice, slander, and *filthy language from your lips* (Colossians 3:8 italics added).

Because these are improper for God's holy people. Nor should there be obscenity, foolish talk or coarse joking, which are out of place (Ephesians 5:3-4).

Put away perversity from your mouth; keep corrupt talk far from your lips (Proverbs 4:24).

I attend a secular university and am constantly dismayed at the cursing which is so commonplace among the students there. But what really appalls me is when I hear some of these same words spewing from my own lips.

We become desensitized to sin when exposed to it on a regular basis. Yet, as Paul tells us in 1 Corinthians 5:10 we cannot disassociate ourselves from the world for if we did, how would anyone ever hear the life changing message of Jesus Christ. Instead, we simply need to remember that while we are *in* the world, we are not *of* the world; there is a big difference.

Raunchy language from the lips of we who claim the Name of Christ cannot be excused. If we wallow in the world's filth, then to whom shall the seekers turn? They will not be able to distinguish those with the light from those in the dark.

Living as children of light takes a conscious effort on our part *and* the help of the Holy Spirit. I have found that praying specifically about my tendency to mutter "four letter" words and staying close to God goes a long way in helping me to put away such perversity from my mouth.

How about you? Is your language out of place?

For further reflection:
Read what James 3:2-12 and James 4:7 says about taming the tongue.

WHAT'S IN A NAME?

You shall not misuse the name of the Lord your God, for the Lord will not hold anyone guiltless who misuses His name (Exodus 20:7).

If you do not carefully follow all the words...which are written in this book, and *do not revere this glorious and awesome name— the Lord your God*—the Lord will send fearful plagues on you (Deuteronomy 28:58 italics added).

But I tell you that men will have to give account on the day of judgment for every careless word they have spoken (Matthew 12:36).

My name is Juanita Louise Wilson Thouin. So what? Yet those strange sounding words, each strung together to form the whole, represent who I am . . . who I've come to be known as. And it is that appellation which is recorded in the Book of Life.

God's name is multifaceted as well: God, Lord, Jesus Christ, and Holy Spirit—just to name a few. He sums up His identity by calling Himself the great "I am".

A name is something to be respected; in God's case it must be revered. I tend to get a little put off when someone just misspells or mispronounces my name. God's name is so worthy of respect that its misuse is deemed a sin.

Humanity's morality stands and falls on our willingness to recognize and fear The Creator. When God's name no longer evokes a sense of awe—when we use it as a curse word or in a flippant manner—we cross from light to darkness and blindly follow Satan's path to destruction.

The third commandment should not to be taken lightly. Using God's name in vain is not just some bad habit or social norm. It is sin—subject to God's swift and terrible judgment.

Are you falling for Satan's crafty plan?

For further reflection:
At the judgment, what does Jesus say He will do with those who are lukewarm? Read Revelation 3:14-22.

——*mm*—

STOP PULLING MY WEIGHT!

What you are doing is not good. You and these people who come to you will only wear yourselves out. The work is too heavy for you; you cannot handle it alone . . . select capable men from all the people . . . and appoint them as officials over thousands, hundreds, fifties and tens. Have them serve as judges for the people at all times, but have them bring every difficult case to you . . . that will make your load lighter, because they will share it with you (Exodus 18:17-22).

For even when we were with you we gave you this rule: "If a man will not work, he shall not eat" (2 Thessalonians 3:10).

Do not let any unwholesome talk come out of your mouths, but only what is helpful for building others up according to their needs, that it may benefit those who listen (Ephesians 4:29).

I really detest group projects; without fail, there's been at least one freeloader in each of my groups. However as long as educators deem them beneficial, I guess we're stuck with these "learning ventures".

After three project experiences I'd like to pass along the following hard learned lessons.

- Group projects only work properly when each member pulls his/her own weight.
- Forcing others to assume our share of the work is not only a poor witness for Christ but also a behavior deserving rebuke.
- Some of us are naturally gifted in areas where others are not. He to whom God gives much, much is required (see Luke 12:48). Assigning tasks to those most qualified tends to increase the group's productivity. i.e. the English majors generally do a good job of typing the report. The Pre-Law majors or computer gurus make great researchers, etc., etc.
- Again, group projects only work properly when each member pulls his/her own weight. Professors expect *each* student to contribute to the work as a whole and thus learn something in the process. When one student becomes a control freak and monopolizes the entire project, everyone looses.
- If a man will not work, he shall not eat. A student's grade ought to reflect the effort put forth. The professor and God expects us to respond honestly on project review sheets. Remember however, when critiquing someone who failed to pull his/her own weight, there's a big difference between scathing criticism and gentle rebuke.
- Finally, throughout the entire endeavor we must clothe ourselves with kindness, compassion, humility, gentleness, and patience, as is fitting for a child of God (see Colossians 3:12-14). Never forget, actions speak louder than words.

For further reflection:
Interested in spiritual growth? Try praying Colossians 1:9-12.

~~~~

HEART ATTACK?

But I tell you that men will have to give account on the day of judgment for every *careless* word they have spoken (Matthew 12:36 italics added).

A wise man fears the Lord and shuns evil, but a fool is hotheaded and *reckless* (Proverbs 14:16 italics added).

My son, preserve sound judgment and discernment, do not let them out of your sight (Proverbs 3:21).

Thom made plans to visit Suzanne, who lived several states away from his college; the two met during summer break. However, while enroute, Thom grew apprehensive about becoming more deeply involved in a long distance relationship. (And enchanted with the two female students with whom he'd bummed a ride.) Finally, just a couple of hours before his expected arrival, Thom phoned, gave some lame excuse, and canceled the visit.

The next day Thom began to suffer from heart palpitations. Two days later, the heart flutters were occurring so often that he went to see a physician. Tests revealed no abnormalities or illness; the diagnosis—stress.

Thom's reason for canceling his visit may have, in part, been based upon legitimate concerns. (Following through may have stoked a fire he could not realistically attend to.) However, Suzanne (and her parents) had made preparations to host a guest in their home and Thom's response to a momentary whim was not only blatantly rude but extremely inconsiderate as well. At the very least, these kind people deserved a serious, honest, explanation for his change of plans.

Irresponsibility comes in many forms: rash decisions, thoughtless comments, unruly behavior, and reckless choices. Behind each of them we find an unwillingness to make sound judgments based on God's principles of respect, honesty, and integrity.

After coming to terms with his irresponsible behavior, Thom's heartbeat returned to normal. He later wrote a letter of explanation and apology to both Suzanne and her parents.

What about you? Do you respect the feelings, property, and time of others? Do you stand by your word? Can you be trusted?

For further reflection:
Sometimes we attempt to rationalize our actions or words. But, by what standard does God judge those same actions and words? Read 1 Kings 8:39.

---wm---

DATE RAPE

If a man happens to meet a virgin who is not pledged to be married and rapes her and they are discovered, he shall pay the girl's father fifty shekels of silver. He must marry the girl, for he has violated her. He can never divorce her as long as he lives (Deuteronomy 22:28-29).

If a man happens to meet in a town a virgin pledged to be married and he sleeps with her, you shall take both of them to the gate of that town and stone them to death—the girl because she was in a town and did not scream for help, and the man because he violated another man's wife. You must purge the evil from among you (Deuteronomy 22:23-24).

It is God's will that you should be sanctified: that you should avoid sexual immorality; that each of you should learn to control his own body in a way that is holy and honorable, not in passionate lust like the heathen, who do not know God; and that in this matter no one should wrong his brother or take advantage of him (1 Thessalonians 4:3-5).

My heart grieves. Becky, a bubbly, bright, freshman at a Christian college recently suffered the horror of date rape. Apparently, Becky had been spending a lot of time at the guys' dorm just goofing around with a group of girl and guy friends; a couple of times, everyone just sacked out for the night rather than trudging back to their own rooms in the wee hours of the morning. Unfortunately, one of Becky's so-called guy friends took advantage of the situation and finding an opportune moment, forced himself upon her. The rest of the story is a living nightmare.

Date rape happens often enough on or near the campus of my secular university that although such goings on still horrify me, I'm no longer surprised. (It usually occurs in conjunction with alcohol.) But hearing about this crime being perpetrated by someone who professes Christianity* raises some startling questions. Have young men, who claim to follow Christ, bought into the world view that sex outside of marriage is acceptable—forced or not? And even though all rape is an abomination unto God, are Christian women forgetting to be wise in their actions? (see Matthew 10:16).

Whatever the reason for this crime's rampart increase, God considers it a violation against mankind and an evil which must be purged from society. As painful as it may be, women please do not let any man get away with this type of assault. Although going to authorities can never erase what happened, it may prevent others from suffering the same fate. Likewise ladies, if any man ever tries to force himself upon you, scream at the top of your lungs. No matter if he's your best friend, your fiancée, your employer, or a relative—scream!

To males and females alike, remember: there is no such thing as date rape—only rape!

For further reflection:
For a graphical reminder of what happens to those who perpetrate evil against others read Revelation 20:10-15.

---

* Not everyone who attends a Christian college is a Christian. However, this young man said that he was.

~~~

THE MASTER SERVANT

Wives submit to your husbands as to the Lord . . . Now as the church submits to Christ, so also wives should submit to their husbands in everything. Husbands, love your wives, just as Christ loved the church and gave himself up for her (Ephesians 5:22–25.)

Jesus called them together and said, "You know that those who are regarded as rulers of the Gentiles lord it over them, and their high officials exercise authority over them. Not so with you. Instead, whoever wants to become great among you must be your servant, and whoever wants to be first must be slave of all (Mark 10:42-44).

When he had finished washing their feet, he put on his clothes and returned to his place. "Do you understand what I have done for you?" he asked them. "You call me 'Teacher' and 'Lord' and rightly so, for that is what I am. Now that I, your Lord and Teacher, have washed your feet, you also should wash one another's feet. I have set you an example that you should do as I have done for you (John 13:12-15).

There they were, standing outside the campus library— "Prophet Daniel" and his wife. She wore a placard which read,

"I'm happy to have my husband as my master" and stood silently, dolefully beside her husband while he preached "the gospel". Whenever a *male* student commented on his teaching, he answered forthrightly. Whenever a *female* student tried to draw this "prophet" into conversation, he pretended the student did not exist. When anyone questioned the wife, she remained dolefully silent.

Obviously, "Prophet Daniel" holds some fairly radical views about the roles of women in marriage and even in society. (I guess he failed to read about Jesus' public conversations with women, see Mark 5:25-29 and 7:24-30.)

The Bible can be likened to a beautiful tapestry. Each thread is perfectly woven together to reveal the character of God, His plan for humanity, and directions for godly living. Only when we gaze upon the masterpiece in its entirety do we fully comprehend the Weaver's design. Separating the individual threads (scripture) from context distorts the pattern and thus corrupts our understanding.

Only when read with its companion verse, Ephesians 5:25, and enlightened by other scripture, can we gain a clear perspective of Ephesians 5:24. Yes, the Creator calls women to recognize their husbands as heads of the home. However, He also calls husbands to love their wives as Christ loved the church. And when we examine Christ's way of loving the church we find that He actually became *her* servant. Wow! "Servant, you make dinner tonight!"

The whole submission issue isn't about a slave/master relationship; it's about mutual respect. For God admonishes all believers to, "clothe yourselves with humility toward one another because God opposes the proud but gives grace to the humble" (1 Peter 5:5).

If "Prophet Daniel" decides to visit your campus, treat him with respect. Then pray that he, and other misguided souls, will put the threads back into the tapestry—and discover the real truth about submission.

For further reflection:

Who else must submit to a higher authority? Read 1 Peter 5:5, Romans 13:1, 1 Corinthians 16:15-16, Hebrews 12:9, Hebrews 13:17, and 1 Peter 2:18.

—*m*—

HEAVE HO!

I can do everything through him who gives me strength
(Philippians 4:13).

Whatever you do, work at it with all your heart, as working for
the Lord, not for men (Colossians 3:23).

Do not be anxious about anything, but in everything, by prayer
and petition, with thanksgiving, present your requests to God
(Philippians 4:6).

I wonder if there is or ever was any student who looks forward to
final exams? After all, sitting at a desk and spitting out a
semester's worth of accumulated "knowledge" (better known as
what can be crammed into the memory bank the night before)
remains the supreme regurgitation experience. If the ultimate goal
of tests is to determine whether or not a student has learned anything wouldn't it be better to give a series of pop quizzes? At least
we wouldn't suffer as much stress. (Until the professor returned
the paper with a less than desirable grade glaring up at us!)

One positive aspect of final exams is that they prepare us for
those difficult occasions that adult life never fails to dish out. After
having experienced both sides of the coin, I can assure you that—

a child with croup, filling out the itemized version of a Federal Income Tax return on April 13 and discovering you've lost the record of your stock transactions, working overtime the night before you are scheduled to catch a plane for a two week vacation and you aren't packed yet, or sweating through a job interview and then having the interviewer tell you a decision won't be made for several days—rate right up there with finals on the pressure gauge.

I have learned (and often the hard way) that the best prescription for getting through high pressure periods is the following:

- Remember that Christ has promised never to leave me nor forsake me and that with His help I can survive.
- Remember that the ultimate goal behind all that I do is to glorify God and with this in mind, to put forth my very best effort.
- Having done number two, by prayer and petition ask God to bless my faithfulness and fill me with the peace that passes all understanding.

For further reflection:
What did Jesus do just hours before He faced the greatest challenge of His life on earth? Read Luke 22:41-43.

—*mm*—

BACK HOME AGAIN

Then all the people left, each for his own home, and David returned home to bless his family (1 Chronicles 16:43).

A cord of three strands is not quickly broken (Ecclesiastes 4:12).

There is a time for everything and a season for every activity under heaven: a time to scatter stones and a time to gather them, a time to embrace and a time to refrain (Ecclesiastes 3:1,5).

We were all excited that first Christmas after Jesse went away to college. Since our oldest son wasn't scheduled to leave for boot camp until the middle of January, we intended to bask in the joys of being a "whole" family again. Lovingly, I vacuumed and polished Jesse's empty room in eager anticipation of his long awaited homecoming. At last he arrived and we all laughed as our dog, Daisy, barking excitedly, alternated between circling Jesse's legs and rolling onto her back to have him scratch her stomach. After the fanfare, the rest of us returned to our normal routines; Jesse unpacked his clothes and stereo and settled in for a month of not having to share a room, only family noise, and Mom's cooking.

It didn't take long, however, for all of us to realize that somehow, our family had changed. Jesse was more independent and often wore a melancholy look. He tried to fit in and pick up the pieces where he'd left off in the fall, but the puzzle had changed. One day, with a pained look on his face he confided, "Mom, I just don't belong here any more. I mean . . . this is my home but it's not my home." Deep down I knew he spoke the truth.

The transition from childhood to adulthood via college is a paradox. You are on your own but then again not on your own; free but not free to make your own choices; a part of your family but not a part of your family. The fact remains, for however long it takes to complete your education, you will find yourself, to waning degrees, vacillating between who you were as a child in your parents' home and who you are becoming as a productive member of society. The former calls for embracing; the latter calls for letting go.

As the semester winds down and you shift back into the embracing mode, mixed feelings may be on the horizon. In due time, however, you *and* your parents will grow more comfortable with the letting go process until eventually, when you embrace . . . it will be as one adult visiting another.

For further reflection:
What kind of home do we all look forward to? Read 2 Peter 3:13.

EPILOGUE

Not many of you should presume to be teachers, my brothers, because you know that we who teach will be judged more strictly (James 3:1).

When I want to do good, evil is right there with me. For in my inner being I delight in God's law; but I see another law at work in me, waging war against the law of my mind and making me a prisoner of the law of sin . . . What a wretched man I am! Who will rescue me . . . ? Thanks be to God—through Jesus Christ our Lord! (Romans 7:21-25).

Not that I have already obtained all this, or have already been made perfect, but I press on to take hold of that for which Christ Jesus took hold of me. Brothers I do not consider myself yet to have taken hold of it. But, one thing I do . . . I press on toward the goal to win the prize for which God has called me heavenward in Christ Jesus (Phillipians 3:12-14).

I am just an ordinary person living an ordinary life. Though I accept the stricter measure of obedience which comes as a result of answering God's call to write this book, like Paul, as long as I remain in this earthly body, I will always be a sinner saved only by the grace of Jesus Christ.

So often we tend to place those who's names grace the covers of books, magazines or albums on pedestals. But, there is only *One* who deserves to be on a pedestal; God the Father, Son, and Holy Spirit. To *Him* be the glory forever and ever. Amen!

THE AUTHOR

Juanita Thouin attends James Madison University in Harrison-burg, VA as a Mass Communication Major. She has participated in the Bible Study Fellowship program for ten years, served on the Board of Trustees for Northern Shenandoah Valley Youth for Christ, led teen Bible study groups, and spent several years as a high-school substitute teacher. The mother of two grown sons, she, along with her husband and teen-age daughter, lives amongst the splendor of the Blue Ridge Mountains.

You may write to Juanita:

c/o Lyrical Legacys, Ltd.
PO Box 152
Woodstock, VA 22664

Or send email to:

jthouin@shentel.net

To order additional copies of

Eight O'Clock Classes
and Other Life-Threatening Situations

send $9.99 plus $3.95 shipping and handling to:

Books, Etc.
PO Box 1406
Mukilteo, WA 98275

or have your credit card ready and call:

(800) 917-BOOK